HIS TO CLAIM

AVA GRAY

Copyright © 2025 by Ava Gray

All rights reserved.

No part of this book may be reproduced in any form or by any electronic or mechanical means, including information storage and retrieval systems, without written permission from the author, except for the use of brief quotations in a book review.

❦ Created with Vellum

ALSO BY AVA GRAY

Contemporary Romance

Scandalously Yours Series

Sinful in Scrubs

A New York Criminal Empire Series

The Irish Redemption

Mafia Kingpins Series

His to Own

His to Protect

His to Win

His to Possess

His to Claim

. . .

The Valkov Bratva Series

Stolen by the Bratva

Kept by the Bratva

Captured by the Bratva

Captivated by the Bratva

Festive Flames Series

Silver Hills' Christmas Miracle

Holly, Jolly, and Oh So Naughty

The Christmas Eve Delivery

Valentine's with the Silver Fox

Harem Hearts Series

3 SEAL Daddies for Christmas

Small Town Sparks

Her Protector Daddies

Her Alpha Bosses

The Mafia's Surprise Gift

The Billionaire Mafia Series

Knocked Up by the Mafia

Stolen by the Mafia

Claimed by the Mafia

Arranged by the Mafia

Charmed by the Mafia

Alpha Billionaire Series

Secret Baby with Brother's Best Friend

Just Pretending

Loving The One I Should Hate

Billionaire and the Barista

Coming Home

Doctor Daddy

Baby Surprise

A Fake Fiancée for Christmas

Hot Mess

Love to Hate You - The Beckett Billionaires

Just Another Chance - The Beckett Billionaires

Valentine's Day Proposal

The Wrong Choice - Difficult Choices

The Right Choice - Difficult Choices

SEALed by a Kiss

The Boss's Unexpected Surprise

Twins for the Playboy

When We Meet Again

The Rules We Break

Secret Baby with my Boss's Brother

Frosty Beginnings

Silver Fox Billionaire

Taken by the Major

Daddy's Unexpected Gift

Off Limits

Boss's Baby Surprise

CEO's Baby Scandal

Playing with Trouble Series:

Chasing What's Mine

Claiming What's Mine

Protecting What's Mine

Saving What's Mine

The Beckett Billionaires Series:

Love to Hate You

Just Another Chance

Standalone's:

Ruthless Love

The Best Friend Affair

. . .

PARANORMAL ROMANCE

Maple Lake Shifters Series:

Omega Vanished

Omega Exiled

Omega Coveted

Omega Bonded

Everton Falls Mated Love Series:

The Alpha's Mate

The Wolf's Wild Mate

Saving His Mate

Fighting For His Mate

Dragons of Las Vegas Series:

Thin Ice

Silver Lining

A Spark in the Dark

Fire & Ice

Dragons of Las Vegas Boxed Set (The Complete Series)

Standalone's:

Fiery Kiss

AVA GRAY

Wild Fate

BLURB

One forbidden night. One deadly kidnapping. One virgin who doesn't realize she's already been marked as his.

ARCHER

I've spilled blood for money and buried my conscience alongside the bodies of my enemies.

When a mysterious beauty in a lace mask slides her tongue against mine at a masquerade ball, something primal awakens inside me—a possessive hunger I thought I'd killed years ago.

Then she's snatched by thugs right in front of me, and I discover she's Carlotta Rossi—virgin sister to the most ruthless mafia family in New York. The same family that's paying me to keep them alive.

Now she's under my protection in my remote cabin, sleeping in my bed, her tempting curves just inches away. I should keep my hands to myself. I've been hired to guard her body, not claim it.

But the moment she trembles beneath my touch, I know the truth—she was mine from our first kiss. And I'll burn down the world before I let anyone take what's mine.

Even if claiming her means signing my own death warrant.

CARLOTTA

I'm tired of being the sheltered Rossi princess, the virgin sister everyone underestimates.

When a dangerously seductive stranger pins me against the wall at a masquerade ball, his talented mouth making promises his body is desperate to keep, I feel truly seen for the first time.

Instead, I end up kidnapped by my family's worst enemy, a man who wants to hang me as bait to destroy everyone I love.

My mysterious masked lover turns out to be Archer—the deadly, brooding mercenary my brothers trust to save me. Now I'm trapped alone with him in his cabin, and the way he looks at me makes my body burn hotter than sin.

He warns me to stay away. Says my brothers would kill him. Says he's too damaged, too dangerous.

But I see the way his eyes follow me—possessive, hungry, determined. Like I already belong to him.

And the terrifying truth? I want nothing more than to be his to claim.

His to Claim is book five of the Mafia Kingpins series. This scorching-hot standalone features: possessive alpha, virgin heroine, forced proximity, only one bed, brother's friend, surprise

pregnancy, and enough heat to make a confession booth burst into flames!

1

CARLOTTA

Leaning forward, I apply more eyeliner and smudge it beneath my lashes. It's Thursday night which means it's girls' night out and, for the first time since we started the tradition, I'm not looking forward to meeting up with Alessia, Hannah, Gabriella and Blake. Even though I love them like sisters, lately it's been a little hard for me to be around them.

I guess what it boils down to is I feel left out. And a little jealous. Okay, *a lot* jealous.

My older brothers and their significant others are all gloriously, sickeningly happy and head over heels in love with each other. As fabulous as that is for them, well, for me…it's been quite lonely lately.

Whether I like it or not, I'm the last one standing. The only single sibling left and the youngest sister of the powerful Rossi family.

With a heavy sigh, I lift the mascara wand and sweep it over my long lashes, wondering why that is. Studying my reflection in the mirror with a critical eye, I wonder for the millionth time what's wrong with me? Not to be arrogant, but I'm doing okay in the looks department. Sure, I get self-conscious sometimes like every other female out there, but I know I'm blessed with good Italian genes—long, thick dark brown hair, even darker eyes, a permanent bronze tone to my skin. And despite all the pasta I manage to eat, I'm able to keep my figure and my curves are in all the right places.

And that leads me to start questioning other things—things that aren't very easy to fix. Do I have a bad personality? Is that why men seem to keep their distance? Do I have a resting bitch face? I don't think so, I decide, looking at my reflection. Maybe it's my sassy personality that scares them away. Angelo does call me a firecracker sometimes.

Lately, it seems like I've been questioning a lot of things, especially decisions I've made in the last few years. All, of course, which have led me to this point—painfully alone.

Maybe it's because Angelo, my closest brother, just got married and he's the one I thought I could always count on to remain single. Ang had always declared he'd be a bachelor to the day he died, swore it up and down, and I believed it. We all did. He's far too good-looking, beyond charming and used to say serious relationships were to be avoided at all costs and just the idea of one made him break out in hives.

So much for that.

Blake, a bounty hunter, accidentally kidnapped him instead of her intended target and the rest, as they say, is history. Last week at the wedding reception, they already announced Blake is pregnant. Talk about a complete and total one-eighty.

Of course, I'm going to love being an aunt…again…and I'm genuinely happy for my brothers, their wives and their children.

I think it must be fear of missing out that has me all out of sorts lately. Either that or maybe my biological clock is ticking. *I'm only twenty-five, though,* I remind myself. There's no need to be in a rush to get knocked up. I know people who didn't start their families until they were well into their thirties, even forty nowadays.

I did always have my heart set on being a young mom, though. While I still had the energy and would be able to have my child grow up with all their cousins. Because, let's face it, my brothers and their wives are popping out kids like they're Pez dispensers.

Reaching for the hot curling iron, I pick up a strand of my dark chestnut hair and wind it around the wand, contemplating the root of the problem. It's not that I'm in a hurry to get married and have kids, it's more that I want to start experiencing life. Things like love and sex are mysteries to me.

Very tantalizing mysteries that I want to explore.

As I continue to work my way around my head, curling my normally straight hair, I inevitably think about the one man I did date seriously. Rendall Smith. God, what a jackass. An image of his stupid face pops into my head. Dirty blond hair, greenish eyes, normal height and build. Nothing like my powerhouse brothers.

Rendall was average in every way. Except, of course, when it came to the asshole scale. Then he was off the charts.

God, I still feel so stupid for spending so much time with him, for believing him, for almost giving my virginity to him. What a complete and total waste that would've been. Yes, I want to sleep with a man, but I want him to be a good guy. Or, at least not treat me like shit.

Growing agitated by memories of what happened, my hand slips and the hot iron burns my forehead.

"Ow! Dammit!" I cry. With a frustrated sound, I set it down on the counter with a thunk and stare hard at my reflection in the mirror again.

Maybe it is my looks. Maybe I'm not pretty enough.

God, I hate the self-doubt creeping in, but I can't help it.

Like my brothers, I have dark hair and brown eyes. Well, except for Vin who has the most amazing shade of green eyes which can't be missed or overlooked because they're so stunning. To be honest, I don't usually remember a person's eye color. When I'm talking to someone, especially a man, I tend to look everywhere but in their eyes. For some reason, it makes me incredibly uncomfortable. Maybe because the eyes truly are the window to the soul, and I feel exposed and vulnerable.

Squinting, I try to remember what color Rendall's eyes were—I thought greenish, but now I'm second guessing myself. Maybe they were more brown. Hazel? Or wait, no. Gray. Hmm, I'm not sure. Oh well, it doesn't matter because he is a complete douchebag who I never want to see or run into again.

I lightly trace a finger over the red burn mark that now mars my forehead and frown. *Nice.* Grabbing some concealer, I lightly cover it as best as I can then check the time on my phone. I should leave in ten minutes, so I head into my bedroom to get dressed.

My apartment is small and cute and located in Greenwich Village. While my brothers live in much bigger and fancier homes, I like my cozy place. It fits me. Lately, I've been spending the majority of my time in the corner book nook I put together, lost in romance novels. It consists of a big, overstuffed chair near the window so there's plenty of natural light, a floor lamp if I need it, and floor to ceiling shelves that I had Vin help me install. I love reading, and I spent days organizing my paperback collection by series and by authors. Lately, it's the one thing that gives me absolute joy—curling up in my teal chair, sipping flavored coffee from my favorite mug and reading about falling in love.

Because I figure it's that or nothing. What can I say? It's a sad state of affairs.

I think part of the reason I feel lost is because I'm not exactly sure what I should be doing with my life. My parents live in Sicily on a vineyard and our family owns a successful wine company, Rossi Vineyard, and Vincentius runs the day to day operations. Miceli, my oldest brother, handles the mafia side of things and has his fingers in everything. He's practically the Don of New York City and runs everything. Nothing gets past him. And Enzo is a genius when it comes to stocks and investments. That man makes so much money, he could probably buy this entire city and everyone in it.

Angelo has always been more like me. Not quite sure of his purpose, but now that he's found Blake, he seems so happy, so utterly content.

But me… I've been struggling lately trying to figure out where I belong and I'm just not sure. I'm much more creative than my business-minded brothers, but when I think about a career and what I want to do for the next thirty or forty years, I come up blank.

It's a good thing money isn't an issue or I'd be back home living with my parents in Sicily. But since they've made my brothers and I all shareholders in the company, money gets deposited into all of our accounts every quarter. The wine makes a fortune and then I let Enzo play with it and he makes me more money.

So money isn't an issue. But love and finding something I'm good at seems to be my biggest problem. More than anything, I would love to find my person and find my place. As corny as it sounds, I feel like I'm not fulfilling my destiny, that I'm not doing whatever it is I'm supposed to be doing.

I just wish I knew what that was exactly.

After slipping on a little black dress and heels, I grab my purse and head out. It's good for me to get out of the house and I do enjoy chatting with my sisters-in-law. Maybe they can help me figure my life out. Because right now, I feel lost. More lost and confused and lonely than I ever have before.

Raising a hand, I flag down a yellow taxicab and hop inside. I tell him the name of the cute little restaurant where we're meeting and settle back in the seat and scroll through my phone. Traffic is always a nightmare at this time of night, so I get comfortable and settle in.

Luckily, the place we're meeting isn't too far away and, once we arrive, I pay the fare and hop out. Even though everyone is always Ubering nowadays, I still like my crusty, old school NYC cabs. Guess I'm classic like that.

My heels click against the polished wooden floor as I walk into the trendy restaurant and see my girls already gathered at a corner table. I wave and make my way over to the very fertile group of women. Alessia and Miceli are awaiting baby number two already and she looks ready to pop. Hannah and Gabriella gave birth not long ago and are still nursing their new little bundles of joy. And Blake looks slim as ever, but she's a couple of months along. My brothers are ridiculously virile. It's not something I like to think about too hard, so I push it out of my mind fast before I accidentally envision something that I don't want to ever picture.

"Hello, beautiful mamas," I say in greeting and sit down. I immediately flag a waiter over, needing some alcohol in my system. "Can I get a cosmo?"

He nods and walks off.

"Not a mama yet," Blake states, sliding a hand over her flat stomach.

"It'll be here before you know it," Gabriella tells her with a knowing smile.

"How was the honeymoon?" I ask Blake. She and Ang just got back not long ago. After getting married, he flew them up to Maine in his helicopter where they stayed in a little, cozy cabin. My brother likes to show off his piloting skills, but he's damn good. I think he missed his calling as a Navy pilot.

"Amazing," she answers dreamily. "Going back to where we fell in love was really special."

"Aww, we're so happy for you," Alessia says, and everyone nods.

A minute later, the conversation inevitably turns to babies and motherhood. They're all new moms and I understand they're learning a lot from each other, but I immediately feel left out. So I just smile and nod and down my drink then quickly order another one.

I don't have much to contribute to the conversation and, eventually, I'm staring off into space, wondering if I'll ever be able to join in and offer some useful or valid piece of advice about being married or having kids. After a while, Blake and Gabriella seem to pick up on my silence.

"Okay, enough about babies," Gabriella states, and I send her a grateful look. "Just so you know, Carlotta, as the only single woman at this table, we're all a little jealous."

"Jealous?" I echo in disbelief. "Of what?"

"Your freedom, for one," Blake says.

"Having the world at your feet," Alessia says.

"And being able to go off and do whatever you want, whenever you want," Hannah adds.

"I don't feel very lucky," I say a little glumly, but I suppose they have a point. "In fact, if I'm being honest, I'm a little envious of you guys. Okay, more than a little."

There's such a wistfulness in my voice and I can't even try to hide it.

"You're so crazy happy," I continue, "and, don't get me wrong, I'm so very happy for you. I just…I don't know what's wrong with me. Lately, I've just been a little…"

My voice trails off and they're all listening with rapt attention.

"A little what?" Alessia asks gently.

"Lonely," I admit in a quiet voice. Then I quickly add, "But I know it's my fault. I don't go out as much as I should and I have a hard time trusting men."

"I was the same way," Blake says. "It's a miracle Angelo and I ever met. My entire life had been work and I never went out. Not socially, anyway. Just to hunt down bad guys."

I smirk, imagining Blake as a bounty hunter in her former life. Now that she's married and expecting, she doesn't run around and capture dangerous people any longer. Mostly because Angelo would have a heart attack.

"So let's change that," Hannah says easily, a glimmer in her eyes. "Girls, I think we should help Carlotta find a good man."

"Do any exist?" I can't help but ask.

"Yes," Alessia answers without hesitation. "Your brothers."

"Well, I can't date my brothers nor would I want to—no offense—so where are the rest of the good men?" I wonder aloud. Because I sure as hell can't find any.

"Out there, somewhere," Hannah says, which is completely unhelpful. "And we're going to help you find one."

"Thanks, and not to burst your bubble, but the situation looks pretty grim, ladies."

"Oh, c'mon," Gabriella scoffs, waving her hand through the air. "You're still a baby. You have plenty of time. Something or someone definitely made you a little jaded, though."

Gabriella definitely doesn't miss a thing. Although being a business woman and being married to Enzo, I can understand how she'd always be on her toes. She is extremely perceptive, quite intuitive and wise beyond her years.

"Yeah, his name was Rendall and in a matter of three months, he managed to shatter my self-esteem and trust in the opposite sex. Now I'm scared I'll never be good enough for anyone or be able to trust a man again."

"Oh, sweetie, not all men are like that. The best ones will love and protect you. Always," Alessia tells me, and the other women nod.

"That's right," Hannah agrees. "Vin saved me when I needed someone the most."

Vincentius had stepped in and rescued Hannah when she'd been forced to participate in an underground auction. He'd outbid everyone else, swooped in and carried Hannah out of that nightmare. Literally, in his arms, he'd marched up to the stage, lifted her up and carried her away.

"You can't give up on love." Alessia reaches over and lays a hand on my arm. "We'll help you, won't we, ladies?"

They all nod.

"I have an idea," Gabriella declares, the corner of her mouth lifting. "The masquerade!"

"What about it?" I ask, not catching on.

There's a masquerade party benefit happening this weekend, but I wasn't planning on going. I don't have a costume or a date, and it all seems like way too much effort.

"Yes!" Alessia grins, nodding. "You have to come, Carlotta."

I start to shake my head, but then realize that maybe they're right. I keep saying I need to get out more and this would definitely check that box. The masquerade is a big event and it will draw a big crowd. Maybe a handsome, single stranger? I guess I can hope. Above all, though, it's an important charity event and showing support would be a good thing to do.

Still though, I am not entirely convinced. Plus, I'm still feeling down and not good enough or confident enough to snag a man's attention. My flirting has gotten rusty.

"I don't have anything to wear," I tell them. It's a lame excuse, I know.

"We can help," Hannah declares without hesitation, and the girls nod in agreement.

After briefly hesitating, I slowly nod. "Why the hell not?" I say, and they all squeal.

The truth is, I'm a romantic at heart, so I'll give it a try. Maybe, if fate is smiling down on me, I'll meet someone and kickstart my love life.

I won't hold my breath, though.

2

ARCHER

Leaning back in my black leather chair, I lift my feet and prop them up on the edge of my desk. I'm not sure how much faith I have in the conversation that just took place with one of my informants, but I'm weighing all the intel in my head. Deciding if it's worth my time to look into it more deeply.

It involves Miceli Rossi and his family. Normally, I wouldn't worry because I know Miceli can take care of himself and his people. But a lot has happened to his family lately and I've been keeping an ear open. If I come across any information that can help or, in this case, warn him, I pass it along.

To be clear, I owe him nothing; he owes me nothing.

Although, technically, I suppose Miceli does owe me, but I told him not to worry about it. Owing me is like owing the devil. No one wants to go there. I've seen things, done things, know things…that no one else should. Or, would ever want to be aware of because they're dark and deadly secrets.

I have my pulse on the underworld and make it my business to know what's happening in the city at all times. If a threat arises, I handle it.

My league of informants, mostly a web of criminals, keep me in the loop. I also have contacts in the police department and stay on good terms with a former CIA agent.

So when I say I know what's happening, well, it's a bit of an understatement. I'm like the TMZ of the NYC underworld. I get the gossip and the facts first, and then I decide how best to use that information. Who to tell, who not to tell—and who will pay the most to learn what I know.

While I rule the underworld, Miceli Rossi, on the other hand, rules the mafia kingdom. Along with the other five ruling families who made their way over from Italy and Sicily generations ago, they run the city's businesses. While he rules the day, I rule the night.

After all I've done and seen, it's where I belong—in the darkness.

I live a solitary life and that's how I prefer it. I have no desire to ever meet a woman, get married and have a family. Darkness consumes every aspect of who I am, where I've been and where I'm going. There's no room in my life for innocence. Besides, I'd probably be allergic and instantly break out in hives if I came in close proximity to anything remotely pure or good.

My attention falls on the invitation sitting on the edge of my desk. It's for a charity masquerade ball and normally I'd ignore it. Run it through my shredder without a second thought. But, in this case, it behooves me to go. The couple holding the event recently reached out to me and asked for my services. I didn't accept or decline yet because I like seeing people in person first, so I can watch how they interact and conduct their business before taking them on as a client. Because, let's face it, the shit I do, that they want me to do, isn't always on the up and up. I need to know I'm working for decent human beings because even the devil has standards. Plus I figure I can also keep a close eye on the Rossi family while I'm there, just in case trouble surfaces. Two birds, one stone kind of thing.

Rumor has it that Carmine Gallo is planning his revenge on the Rossi family and he's willing to do anything to make it happen. Granted, Angelo and company are supposedly responsible for burning the man's mansion down and forcing him to go into hiding because he was being hunted down by bounty hunters. But in all fairness, Gallo had put the original hit out on Angelo and his new wife, Blake Serrano Rossi. They just outsmarted him, flipped the tables, and now he's pissed.

My gaze moves from the invite over to my cell phone, and I snatch it up. After hitting Miceli's number, I lean back further in my chair as it rings. The other man answers almost immediately.

"Archer, how are you?"

"Oh, you know," I respond easily, "same old, same old."

I'd like to say I'm calling Miceli out of the goodness of my heart, but that would be a lie. It's always business and how best I can increase the money in my coffers.

"What have you got for me?" the other man asks, getting straight to the point which is fine with me. I wouldn't necessarily call Miceli Rossi a friend, more of a strategic business acquaintance. It's not like we ever hang out, drink beers and shoot the shit together. No, instead, we deal in information.

And, of course, cold hard cash. Which is exactly the reason for my call. By keeping Miceli informed, which is the best and most priceless thing I can do, he will pay me back generously with favors and money. It's a win-win situation for the both of us.

"I wanted to give you a heads-up," I say, flicking a piece of lint off my black T-shirt. "Gallo is on the warpath and has vowed to bring you and your family down. By any means necessary."

Rossi curses under his breath. "That asshole is becoming a thorn in my side."

"Yeah, well, you might want to make sure he's taken care of sooner rather than later."

"Noted. I appreciate the heads-up. Like always, I'll make sure you're compensated."

I sit up straight, my boots dropping down and hitting the floor with a dull thud. "Good doing business with you, Rossi."

"Same."

We hang up and then I stand up and stretch. Once again, my eyes focus on the invitation and I grab it. It's a black envelope with my name embossed in fancy handwriting on the front. I open it and slide the black card out. All the information for the party is there in silver, foiled writing, including the part where masks and costumes are greatly encouraged.

I sigh. Playing dress-up isn't high on my agenda, but I've heard all about this particular party, so I know that everyone dresses up. In fact, the guests go all out and dress to the nines. No one removes their mask until midnight and it's a tradition that's been going on for the past ten years.

And who am I to break tradition?

Nobody. So that means my ass has to put together a costume. Of course, I'm dreading it and have zero ideas. I also have zero friends to help me figure it out.

Shoving a hand through my black hair, I remind myself it's for the best. Remaining alone and detached is for…the…best. I repeat the phrase to myself a few times, driving it home.

A long time ago, things had been different…and look how horribly that had turned out. No, I refuse to ever endanger anyone ever again. That means I won't bring anyone into my world or allow myself to get too close. Especially to a woman.

Without warning, an image of Caitlin fills my head. My body reacts the same as it always does and nausea pummels my stomach. She didn't deserve what happened to her and no amount of time that has passed has helped ease the weight of my guilt. My grief has lessened over time and that probably just makes me a bigger bastard than I already am.

Truthfully, I don't think I'm capable of love. I've heard about it, read about it, even witnessed it. Hell, the Rossi men have all fallen and now their worlds revolve around their wives. But I can't fathom meeting a woman and having my world tilt and my stomach fill with butterflies. If she's attractive, the only thing I can count on is a hard-on and, if I'm lucky, a one-night stand.

It's all I'm capable of, anyway. When Caitlin died, any humanity and warmth I had died along with her. I'm not a good guy. I'm cold, ruthless and enjoy the power that comes along with information. I'd much rather count the dollars in my various bank accounts around the world than cuddle with some needy woman. Because eventually they all turn needy and want more than I can give.

With another sigh, I walk over to the large picture window that overlooks New York City. The sun set a few minutes ago and the night is upon us. Bright lights glow all around and I take a moment to soak it all in. This city is my domain and I like to keep it clean of vermin and scum.

Maybe that includes you, a little voice taunts.

Shaking my head, I lock all the guilt and doubts away and cross my arms. As a former spec ops guy, I'm good at compartmentalizing. The military also taught me to be tenacious, focused and I learned how to get shit done. It also made me hate showing any kind of weakness. Projecting strength and confidence is key. It's who I am now and there's no going back.

As I gaze out over the city I love, my mind wanders back to Carmine Gallo. He moved here not quite two months ago and instantly started causing problems. From what I can deduce, he's interested in taking over as much here as he can. Word on the street is he was asking a lot of questions about the other mafia families. From what I'm hearing, it sounds like he wants to take over the Five Families alliance. Or, possibly crush it entirely.

Gallo doesn't want to share; he wants all the power and control.

He's a greedy sonofabitch, a threat to the setup here that's working quite nicely lately. I don't want him riling up alliances and creating new enemies. For the first time in a very, very long time—hell, ever— the five powerhouses of this city have found a peace that always seemed to elude them. Gallo needs to be handled and I'm hoping Rossi will get it done. Otherwise, I'll take care of it myself.

In the meantime, I need to figure out a costume for the masquerade party. Not my area of expertise, that's for damn sure. I'm a simple guy and prefer my T-shirt and cargo pants. Comfort is a priority, but I suppose I can suck it up and put on a suit and uncomfortable mask for an hour or two.

There's a black suit in the back of my closet somewhere. The last time I wore it was to Caitlin's funeral almost five years ago. An image of her cream casket decorated with tiny pink roses makes my stomach roil. Some days it seems like just yesterday that she died and other times it feels like forever and a day. But the one constant, the one thing that never changes, is the heavy guilt.

Because if I had been here, if I'd been home to protect her, Caitlin would still be alive.

Okay, enough, I chastise myself. *You have to let it go.*

I wish I could. I really fucking wish I could stop blaming myself, but I can't.

Turning away from the bright lights of the city night, I wander back over to my desk and drop down. The seat squeaks as I maneuver it closer to the desk and my laptop, and I quickly pull up a website and search for a mask. Hundreds and hundreds of options pop up and I honestly don't give two shits. I just need something to cover my face and not draw attention. My plan is to stick to the shadows, like I'm good at doing, and keep an eye on the Rossi family from afar. Of course, I'll make contact with Miceli, let him know I'm there, and he'll deposit a ridiculous sum of money into my bank account. He's grateful like that and it's one of the reasons I keep him up to date on what's happening.

I stop scrolling when a skeleton mask snags my attention. First, I like that it just covers the lower half of my face, not obscuring my eyes. And, second, it's badass as fuck. Creepy, too. I hit buy and choose the overnight delivery option. The masquerade benefit is this weekend so I need to throw this costume together asap. I guess I have it already, though.

That wasn't too hard, I think, sitting back and lacing my fingers.

Now what?

The question flits through my head and I suppose I could kill some time with a beer, a pizza and the newest Netflix drama. My stomach rumbles, reminding me that I haven't eaten dinner yet. The urge to get out of my apartment fills me, though, so I decide to grab that beer and some food down at the corner pub I like to frequent. After holstering my Glock 19 at my back, I slip a jacket on, lock up and leave. I never leave home without my piece concealed somewhere on my body. The military taught me well and without a weapon, I feel naked.

I live in a warehouse apartment on the edge of the Hudson River, not too far away from Greenwich Village. My neighborhood is quieter than the Village, though, and I dig the industrial vibe of my place and being so near the docks.

When you do what I do and have done, it's important to maintain a low profile. I don't like drawing any attention to myself or standing out. I much prefer being a ghost, a shadow who is hard to track down, not easily found or identified. Because even though I have a lot of good connections, I also have endless enemies. People who want to usurp my power and control from me and others. Assholes like Carmine Gallo who need to be kept in their place and dealt with. They need to understand the hierarchy of this city and accept that they're at the bottom of the totem pole.

The walk down to Flannigan's is quick and easy, barely a block from my place. I like it because, although it can get busy, it's never too crowded or too loud. The service is friendly, but not overly so, and the food is good.

As usual, I sidle up to the bar and perch on the end stool in the corner. It allows me to keep my eyes on the other patrons and on all of the exit points. What can I say? Old habits die hard. Jimmy, the usual weeknight bartender, heads over and greets me.

"Hey, there, what can I get you? The usual?" he asks, and I nod.

Although I don't like to get too chummy with anyone, I'm a regular customer here, so it makes it hard to avoid. But Jimmy never asks too many questions and doesn't pry, so I don't mind. The other bartender, Missy, usually works the earlier shift, and even though I've kept my distance and answered her questions with cool, vague answers, she's made it known on more than one occasion that she'd like to get to know me better. A whole lot better. Of course, I had to shoot her down and put an end to that real quick, but the woman is persistent. So, lately, I've avoided coming here when she's working. It's just easier.

A basketball game plays on the large TV, but I ignore it. I've never been overly interested in sports, unless it involved some type of shooting or martial arts. That grabs my attention because I enjoy both. But men running around and throwing balls? Not so much.

Jimmy cracks open a bottle of Heineken and slides it over to me. I order the bangers and mash which I love. It's an Irish dish that consists of jumbo Irish sausages with homemade mashed potatoes and served with baked beans and gravy. Sounds a little disgusting, but it tastes like heaven on a plate.

After scoping out the crowd and not sensing a threat, I take a sip of beer and allow myself to relax. Well, as much as I can relax. I'm always ready to launch into action at a moment's notice and can thank my years on my ghost ops teams for that. Dangerous missions full of enemies instilled that innate readiness and constant vigilance. Sometimes, I think it's a good thing. Other times, I think it's a curse.

But it's who I am: a former operator who chose his career over his woman.

And because of that decision, which will haunt me until the day I die, she is dead and never coming back.

3

CARLOTTA

I'm surrounded by my brother's wives and we're all getting ready together at Miceli and Alessia's place. They live on Billionaire's Row on the 129th floor of the swankiest penthouse I've ever seen. It's extravagant and far too much for me, but the security is top notch, so it reminds me of a fortress. No one is getting in this place that isn't invited.

My sisters-in-law have convinced all of my brothers to dress up—not that it took much cajoling because they're all pussy-whipped—and the girls have spent the last two hours doing each other's makeup, hair and choosing accessories.

A lot of attention has been directed toward me and I think it's sweet that they're so gung-ho about finding me a man tonight. I'm not going to pretend to be cool about it, either, because all day, my nerves have been bouncing around in my belly. I'm not sure why exactly, but I have the strangest premonition that I might just meet someone special.

Of course, I don't want to get my hopes up too high and have them come crashing down all around me after I meet no one and return home alone. But, I'm feeling extremely hopeful and have a good feeling like I haven't had in the longest time. I don't even remember the last time I was this excited to go out. Maybe it's because I get to wear a big, beautiful dress or because I get to hide behind a mask and there's such an element of mystery to the upcoming evening. Whatever it is, I'm ready.

Although Miceli and Enzo have attended the masquerade party benefit in previous years, the rest of us haven't, so it should be a fun evening.

"Wow," Hannah murmurs, stepping back and looking me over. She just adjusted a red ribbon on my dress. "You look stunning, Lottie."

An appreciative flush makes my face turn warm. "So do you," I say. "You all do. How my brothers managed to snag the most beautiful women in New York is beyond me."

Alessia tilts her head and grins. "They are lucky, aren't they?"

The girls all agree with smiles then focus back on me.

"And you look beyond amazing," Alessia states. "I think every male eye is going to be on the Queen of Hearts tonight."

"Thanks, but I'm not going to get my hopes up," I tell them."well, maybe just a little."

"You're going to be a hit," Gabriella predicts, and Blake nods encouragingly, tossing me a wink.

I sure hope so.

Once we're done primping, we all sweep out into the living room and the men whistle and express their appreciation.

"Lookin' good, Lottie," Angelo says, and the rest of my brothers nod.

"Stay close to us," Miceli states, eyeing me with a frown.

"Why?" I ask.

"Because I have a feeling I'm going to have to beat the guys off in order to keep them away from you."

"She doesn't want to keep them away," Alessia informs her husband, but he only grunts in response.

My brothers can be extremely overprotective, but I suppose it's a good thing. Tonight, however, they can lay off. And if they don't? Well, then I guess I'm going to have to sneak away in order to do a little flirting.

"I'll be fine," I assure them, but I don't miss the worried looks they're all exchanging.

Lifting my voluminous skirts, I follow Miceli and Alessia down to his Range Rover. Everyone drives separately, but since I'm a third wheel, I have to tag along with someone. My skirts are way too big to stuff into some of the smaller cars, so I figure my best bet is to get in the SUV so I can spread them out on the backseat.

On the drive over, Miceli tells Alessia and I about a phone call he received from his mysterious friend, Archer. He warned my brother about Carmine Gallo, a ruthless businessman who put Angelo and Blake on something called the Kill List not long ago. They ended up flipping the tables and Blake had every bounty hunter and assassin in the city going after Gallo. Apparently, he's holding a massive grudge and is out to usurp my family's position of power at the table of the Five Families.

I don't get too involved with the mafia side of things. That's Miceli's domain. But things have changed over the last year and now I'm encouraged to attend meetings with the alliance which consists of the five most powerful mafia families in the city—The Rossi's, The Bianchi's, The DeLuca's, The Caparelli's and The Milano's.

At one time, we all had a very strained relationship. There was plenty of strife and rivalry, especially between certain members. But the bad apples have all been weeded out and eliminated. Our families have come to the realization that it's more beneficial to work together than against each other. Plus, no one wants Gallo at the table But I have a feeling he isn't going to give up easily.

All of that is out of my hands, though, and I'll leave it up to my brothers to handle. Or, so I think, at the time.

Once we reach the fancy hotel where the event is taking place, my mouth drops at the long procession of expensive cars waiting in the valet line. "Oh, wow," I murmur, pressing my nose against the glass. "I didn't know this was such a big deal."

"Everyone of importance in this city attends the masquerade," Miceli informs me. "I don't give a shit about kissing ass or rubbing elbows with these people, but my wife likes dressing up." He smiles at Alessia. "Plus, it's for a good cause."

"A very worthy cause," Alessia reiterates. "The Prevention of Child Abuse. And anything we can do to help, we will, Plus, yes, I do love dressing up in a fancy gown. I can't believe you haven't attended yet, Lottie."

I shrug. "No. Tonight will be my first time."

There's no denying the excitement running through my body. Everyone getting out of their cars is dressed to the nines and I love seeing all the costumes. Once we get closer to the drop off point, I place my mask over my face and tie the ribbons at the back of my head. Some people appear to be dressed as characters or following a theme. Kind of like me.

Tonight, I'm dressed up like the Queen of Hearts. A little ironic, I know, but when I saw the gown and matching mask, I couldn't resist. The little twist on the character from Alice in Wonderland has me looking much more glamorous than the short, dumpy, unlikeable queen who screamed "Off with his head!"

My take is much more striking. The crimson and white dress has a sweetheart neckline, sheer lace sleeves and a large skirt covered in red satin hearts. My red lace mask matches perfectly and little red hearts decorate it. I also have a scepter as my prop and I've never felt more regal.

Let's just hope my Prince Charming is in the building.

With that thought swirling through my head, Miceli finally pulls up to the front of the building. My door is opened and a hand helps me out.

"Thank you," I murmur to the attendant, slipping out and fluffing my skirts. I doublecheck that my mask is securely in place then look up at the glowing lobby. There must be a couple hundred people milling around in there and security is everywhere.

The moment has finally come and I pull in a deep breath and follow my oldest brother and sister in law up the steps and through the double, gilded doors. Miceli escorts us over to the ballroom, through the crowd of people, and hands our invitation to one of the masked people standing just outside the massive, floor to ceiling door. With a nod, the man allows us to enter, wishing us an enchanted evening which happens to be the theme.

As I step into the grand ballroom, I suck in a sharp breath, not expecting it to be so elaborately and beautifully decorated. Three enormous chandeliers hang from the tall ceiling, dripping with crystals, and they provide a dim ambience that resembles a bright, full moon. One entire wall is lined with food and I barely have time to blink before a passing waiter hands me a glass of champagne. I take a sip and the bubbles tickle my nose.

There must be a smoke machine hidden somewhere because it looks as though a fog covers the floor and it swirls around the edge of my dress. A band plays jazz music and I glance over to the dance floor which is crowded with masked couples.

Across the way, I see guests bidding on various items in a silent auction and Miceli takes Alessia's hand, tugging her in that direction.

"Time to spend some money for a good cause," he says, but I don't move, still soaking in the incredible atmosphere. "Lottie, are you coming?"

"In a bit. I'm going to check out the food." More specifically, the desserts. A tray of petit fours has caught my eye and I walk over where a dozen trays are filled with the little frosted cakes.

I choose a red and white one and take a bite. *Mmm, delicious.* As the thought rolls through my head and I chew the sweet treat, my eyes land on a tall man standing not too far away, shoulder propped against the wall, arms leisurely crossed, watching me. He's wearing a black suit, black shirt and tie, and a skeleton mask that only covers the bottom of his face. It's creepy, yet sexy at the same time.

Swallowing down my cake, I pretend not to notice. I can feel the weight of his gaze, though, and I can't help but look over. When I meet his dark eyes, he doesn't look away. If anything, his deep espresso eyes seem to grow more intent.

Unmistakable interest flickers through those mesmerizing eyes of his and I can't look away. It's like they're twin black holes, pulling me in, and there's nothing I can do except succumb to his gravity.

Biting my lower lip, somehow I manage to tear my attention away and take a sip of champagne, hoping it'll cool me off. My hand shakes slightly and I can't believe how much that one look is affecting me. Beneath my skirt, I rub my thighs together, unable to miss the slick heat building there.

Who the hell is this guy? I wonder. *And why is he affecting me like this?*

Telling myself to relax and play it cool, I look back over and he's gone. What? Confusion and disappointment flood me and I spin, ready to search the ballroom, when I realize someone has moved up beside me, an arm brushing against mine.

"How are the petit fours?" a deep voice asks, and I look over to see my mysterious skeleton man at my elbow.

Holy shit! How did he move so fast? My heart is pounding like a runaway freight train and I look into his swirling dark eyes. The entire lower half of his face is covered by his mask, so I have no idea if he's smiling or not.

"Delicious," I say. My mask doesn't cover my mouth like his, so I send him my most dazzling smile.

"I'll take your word for it." He reaches out and snags one, lifting the bottom half of his mask and quickly popping the entire thing in his mouth. When he lets out a small moan of approval, I feel my core tingle.

How is it that he's wearing a mask covering half his face, yet he's the most attractive man I've ever encountered?

Maybe because he's managed to snag my attention like no one else. Ever. It could be his height—well over six feet tall—or the way his suit fits his slim, athletic body. Like it was custom-tailored to show off every muscle lurking beneath. Or, it could be his magnetic presence. Whoever he is, he's a man who can't be ignored.

Before I can say anything else, Hannah appears on my other side and taps my shoulder.

"Have you seen Vin?" she asks. "He told me—"

She abruptly stops speaking when she notices the skeleton hottie beside me.

"Oh, sorry. Did I interrupt anything?" She sends me a mischievous smile.

"Actually, I was about to ask the lovely Queen of Hearts if she'd like to dance with me," he says, and my heart trips in my chest.

"Oh," I murmur, slightly flustered, and Hannah gives me a little push, taking my scepter so she can hold it while I dance. "I'd like that."

He offers his arm and I take it, guiding me away from Hannah who grabs my glass. She is nodding like crazy and giving me a thumbs-up sign. *Oh, God, how embarrassing.* I hope he doesn't notice.

Once we reach the crowded, highly-polished, wood dance floor, he pulls me into his strong arms and sweeps me into the sea of dancers. I look up, barely daring to breathe, and meet his dark brown eyes.

I've always had trouble looking into men's eyes for longer than a blink or two. But something about looking into this man's eyes is easier. I have no idea why, but right now, our gazes are locked onto each other and I'm not uncomfortable. In fact, I'd like nothing more than to sink into their very deep, very mysterious depths.

"You're the most beautiful woman here," he tells me in a low voice, and I practically swoon. It's a damn good thing his strong arms are holding me up.

"Thank you. You don't get out much, do you?" I tease.

A hearty laugh bursts from his throat and I like the way his eyes crinkle in the corners.

"Occasionally," he says, and I smile up at him.

I'm dying to know more about him, but I'm so caught up in the moment, of how it feels to be in a pair of strong masculine arms, that I feel a little tongue-tied and a lot intimidated. Plus he smells so ridiculously good that all I can do is inhale his slightly spicy scent and revel in it.

As we continue to stare into each other's eyes, the rest of the world seems to fall away. I find myself moving closer with each pass around the dance floor. Maybe I'm imagining it, but I think he pulls me in tighter, and even though my voluminous skirts separates us, I can still feel our bodies touching.

Neither of us says another word and, for the first time in my life, I know what it feels like to be lost in someone's eyes.

4

ARCHER

As I spin my Queen of Hearts around the dance floor, I can't look away from her gorgeous mocha-colored eyes. There's so much mystery in those chocolate depths and, instead of asking each other a million questions, we're quiet, caught up in the moment, and relishing it.

There's something about her that intrigues me like no other woman has in a very long time. Hell, maybe ever, if I'm being honest. Of course, I'm attracted to her friendly smile and pretty eyes, but she's wearing a mask. I can't even see her face completely, but who am I kidding? I know she's gorgeous underneath that mask and she smells like the sweetest dessert. Like some kind of sugar-dusted flower.

And the way that gown lifts her full breasts and cinches tightly to emphasize her tiny waist is making my body respond. I mentally scold myself to keep it together and not come off like a creep, rubbing his hard-on against her. It's not like I haven't ever seen a beautiful woman before or been in close proximity. But, well, it's been a while since I've allowed myself to indulge and this lovely woman is making me want things. Sexual things. From my experience, though, the more beautiful a woman is, the more trouble she is later.

So, yeah, just because this little beauty has my full attention right now doesn't mean she won't turn out to be a pain in the ass. It's one of the reasons I'm not engaging her in conversation. I just want to enjoy the moment of us being strangers and not knowing anything about each other. I like the mystery of it. The attraction is also undeniable, hot as hell, and once the song ends, I take her hand and spin her right off the dance floor.

Privacy. I need to whisk her off somewhere so we won't be disturbed because I'm dying to know if her soft, pink lips taste as sweet as she smells. I'm willing to bet they do. Guiding her away from the crowd, I head down a quiet hallway off the main ballroom and open the first door I see.

Empty. It looks like some kind of meeting room because there's a long table and ten or so chairs surround it. After closing the door, I turn to my lady in red hearts and pull her back into my arms. This time there's no music. Just the thundering of our hearts as I trace my thumb over her lower lip.

"You're insanely beautiful," I whisper.

"I'm wearing a mask." Her tone is dry, but also a little full of disbelief.

How could she not believe me? She has to know how damn stunning she is, right? Unless…

Well, if she doesn't then this woman is a rare find. Not an ounce of ego to her. That makes me think someone hurt her, made her feel unworthy, and maybe her self-esteem took a hit, getting knocked down a few pegs.

I want to know who hurt her so I can crush him. I would, too, without a second thought. Because this queen should never doubt herself. She's fucking magnificent.

Her lips part slightly and I can see her pulse beating hard in the hollow of her throat. Her breasts rise and fall faster as I close the distance between us, lower my face, and catch her mouth in a kiss.

With a soft sigh, she leans further into me, and I wish I could feel her body against mine better. But all those long, full, damn skirts are in the way.

At first, the kiss is slow and soft. An introduction. But the moment she opens her mouth in invitation and whimpers for more, I give it to her without hesitation. My tongue slides into her mouth and takes control. Exploring everything. Each recess and corner, every soft place. I deepen the kiss and our mouths fuse together. Her hands wrap around my neck and her fingernails lightly scrape the skin there. She makes some kind of soft purring sound and it's sexy as hell.

We're so caught up in each other that I forget about the masks. They're not in the way too much, but I don't think either of us is ready to take them off just yet. Something about staying anonymous, not knowing each other's names, seeing only part of each other's faces, and remaining two strangers attracted to each other and making out is the biggest turn on.

Lust fuels me and I grab her small waist, lift her up and set her down on the wooden tabletop. It's smooth, a nice polished cherry color, and I step forward between her legs, still kissing her. Our mouths have grown more frantic—deep, wet, needy kisses that have me aroused and aching.

Placing my palms flat on the tabletop, not trusting them to touch her, I devour her. But the need to touch her quickly becomes overwhelming and I move my hands onto her thighs. Curling my fingers into the satin skirts, I slowly drag them up to reveal her slender legs.

Her skin is so soft, like velvet, and I curve my hands around her thighs, slide them up and grasp her ass, pulling her to the edge of the table. One step forward and my aching dick meets her satin panties and, holy fuck, it's good. So damn good. She rolls her hips and I grind against her, holding her close, creating a friction that has us both panting for more.

I'm not sure where exactly this is going and it's not like I have a condom in my jacket pocket. I don't normally start making out with complete strangers, but goddamn, this woman feels like more than a mere stranger. Something about her feels almost familiar. I'm sure that's complete bullshit and just my hormones talking, but whatever. I'm going to dry hump her until I can't take another second. Until I'm on the verge of blowing. Because the alternative is letting her walk away and I'm not ready to do that yet.

Just because I can't slide my aching dick inside her doesn't mean I can't pleasure her more, though. Releasing her plump ass, I round my hands over her thighs, spreading them further. Then I glide a hand between her legs and touch the center of her panties. A little gasp escapes her and she briefly tenses, but then relaxes. I trail a finger over her satin-covered slit. Fucking drenched.

Pure masculine satisfaction makes my chest puff out a little and I move the soaked material aside and touch her wet folds, continuing to stroke her. Her breaths are coming hard and fast now and when I sink a finger inside her wet pussy, her inner muscles clench and her hips begin moving against my hand.

"You like that?" I ask huskily, and she makes an incoherent sound as I add another finger, scissoring them. "Damn, you're tight, sweetheart. So tight and so wet."

I begin to kiss the side of her neck and she drops her head back with a little moan. She's so responsive and I'm loving it. Her legs try to squeeze closed, but I nudge them open with my knee, forcing them further apart.

"No time to be shy now, my masked beauty. Take what you need. Ride my hand until you come," I encourage her.

Our eyes lock and her hips begin moving faster as I thrust my fingers in and out.

"Oh, God," she rasps, nails digging into my arms. She's clutching onto me for dear life.

I plunge my fingers a little deeper, then coat my thumb in her juices and circle her clit. With just the right amount of pressure, she fractures in my arms, a soft cry erupting from those pretty red lips.

With my fingers still inside her slick channel, I can feel her muscles spasming, and I kiss her hard. A sudden knock at the door startles us both and we jerk apart. The red haze of lust lifts fast as I stand up straight, pulling her dress back down with one hand and licking my fingers clean.

She hops off the table just as the door opens and a man in a devil mask appears. "Oh, sorry," he says. "I didn't realize anyone was in here."

He makes a quick exit, dragging a giggling masked woman with him, and I let out a low breath, and turn back to my Queen of Hearts. Suddenly, I'm desperate to know her name. The urge to know everything about her fills me, but I also need to do what I came here to do —meet my potential new client and keep an eye on the Rossi family. So far, I've been a little preoccupied.

"I have a couple of things I need to do," I tell her, glancing down at my watch. Holy hell, how has an hour gone by already? Reluctant to let her go, I grab her hand. "You aren't leaving any time soon are you?"

"No," she whispers.

"Good. Meet me outside at the fountain in a half an hour, okay?"

She nods. "Okay."

I press a kiss to her knuckles.

"What's your name?" she asks softly, tilting her head. Big, dark curls spill over her shoulder and a fresh wave of need pulses through me.

"I'll tell you at the fountain," I promise, suppressing my desire. Even though I don't want to, I release her hand then turn and walk away from the most beautiful distraction I've ever had the good fortune of encountering. Pausing at the door, I glance over my shoulder and see her fixing her mask which is slightly crooked. "Half an hour."

"Right."

With a firm nod, I make my exit even though it pains me. And, yeah, I'm in a lot of discomfort so the first thing I do is head straight into the men's bathroom and get my dick under some semblance of control. The last thing I want to do is walk back into the party with an erection the size of Texas. After mustering up the most unpleasant, least sexy thoughts possible, my dick simmers down.

After washing my hands, I straighten my skeleton mask then head out to track down Derek Travers who asked me for some help. Depending on the read I get and the vibes he gives off, I may or may not decide to take him on and help him out. I'm good at reading people and don't like wasting my time on assholes.

With thoughts of meeting back up with my scorching Queen of Hearts in less than half an hour, I search out Travers and we end up having a good conversation. He's former military and straightforward. A no bullshit kind of guy. We go over the specifics of what he needs and I agree to help him.

Okay, one thing done and one thing left on the agenda. My gaze sweeps the crowd for Miceli Rossi and I spot him and his wife near the dessert table where I ran into my mystery woman earlier. I also keep scanning the ballroom for her, but I don't see her anywhere.

A flash of disappointment fills me, but I push it aside and stroll over and greet Miceli. I like being in his good graces for a number of reasons and maintaining a healthy, communicative relationship is mutually beneficial for the both of us. I don't share a lot with him on the personal front, but that's just me. While he is more of an open book, I'm definitely the closed book. Opening up isn't something I know how to do. It's probably why I didn't reveal my name yet to my mystery woman.

But I'm going to tell her out at the fountain. In fact, a part of me is looking forward to discovering her name, too. Which is strange because normally I don't care. I've slept with women and not known their names. Never even bothered to ask. Why would I, though? I don't do relationships and I always make it perfectly clear upfront. I'm a loner. Giving more than a night or two of myself to a woman is unprecedented...and impossible.

However, for some inexplicable reason, I am absolutely entranced by a total stranger. It's bizarre and I'm having a little trouble wrapping my head around it. I'm normally a level-headed kind of guy who normally doesn't walk around with his head in the clouds, lusting after a particular woman. Yeah, it's been a few months since I've had any action, so that could be it. Or, maybe it's because she is the loveliest creature I've ever met and she intrigues me like no one else. The instant attraction is insane and like nothing I've ever experienced, and I need to find out more about her.

Miceli and I discuss Carmine Gallo and he's becoming a bigger threat every day. I keep checking my watch, counting down the seconds, and he notices.

"Am I keeping you from something?" Miceli asks.

I give my head a shake. "Sorry. I'm just a little distracted tonight."

"Anything I can help with?"

"No, just an upcoming meeting. But, thanks."

"Well, don't let me keep you. If you hear anything else about Gallo, let me know."

"I will."

After a quick nod to him and Alessia, I grab two glasses of champagne from a passing waiter and head toward the large back doors that exit out onto a garden patio with a large fountain and plenty of private nooks for canoodling.

I'm right on time and eagerly counting down the seconds and distance that separate us. I'm ready to unmask her, share some champagne and talk beneath the stars. But when I step out onto the spacious cobblestone patio, my gaze zeroes in on the fountain.

She isn't there.

Disappointment floods me and I look down at my watch for the hundredth time. It's been over thirty minutes and she isn't here.

Okay, relax, I tell myself. *You're acting like a damn stalker. Give the woman a minute.*

More than likely, she got held up by a party guest. I'm still disappointed, though, because I rushed out here to get to her and she's nowhere in sight. Maybe I misread our chemistry. I don't know, she seemed to like coming on my hand.

Am I just a fool, falling under her spell? That's only happened once before and it didn't end well. I'm a dangerous man and loving me can only lead to ruin—like it did with Caitlin.

Maybe it's best that I never see my Queen of Hearts again. For her own safety.

And, hell, for my own sanity because she has my head spinning.

5

CARLOTTA

Five Minutes Earlier...

My head is spinning and it's not because of the bubbly. I'm not exactly sure how to explain what happened almost a half an hour ago and I'm still a little in shock, and pulsing, from the complete stranger who gave me an orgasm.

What in the world is wrong with me? I've never done anything so reckless—or exciting—before. A little thrill shoots through me as I step out onto the back patio. The entire area is surrounded by trees, flowers and plants. In the center of it all is the fountain. Fairy lights hang everywhere and it feels like I just stepped into a magical fairyland.

I know I'm five minutes early, but I can't help myself. I've never been so excited to see someone before and I am absolutely dying to unmask my skeleton man and find out his true identity. Earlier, I had a feeling something amazing was going to happen tonight and, so far, this evening has exceeded my expectations in every possible way.

Picturing the handsome stranger's dark brown eyes, so expressive and mysterious, I walk over and stare at the flowing water falling into the pool. It fills the surrounding air with a soft gurgling sound. It's soothing, almost mesmerizing, and I sigh softly as a breeze brushes across my face, lightly rustling my skirts.

No one is out here since the masquerade party is currently in full swing. Plus, it's a little chilly out and I rub my arms, lost in thought. I still can't believe how wanton I was, how I allowed a complete stranger to kiss and touch me so intimately. That was my first official orgasm given to me by a man and it was so damn good. I can't believe what I've been missing out on all these years. It was way better than the ones I've given myself, that's for damn sure.

Even though I dated Rendall for a few months, I never let him touch me like that. We made out, sure, but other than some kissing and light groping, I kept him at a distance. He never slid a hand down my panties or finger-fucked me into sweet oblivion like my masked man. He might've tried, but I never gave him the opportunity. I think in my heart, I knew he was bad news and that he'd cheat on me. So I was always wary, kept my guard up, and never allowed myself to fully trust him. So, of course, I also didn't get overly intimate with him.

It's a good thing, too. Although he hurt my feelings, I wasn't devastated or destroyed by his infidelity. Sadly, I expected it. There was something about him that rubbed me the wrong way and wouldn't allow me to get too close.

My subconscious must've known he was a cheating dick before my conscious mind did.

Either way, I got over him easier than maybe I should have. But since it was such a bad experience, I pulled back from the dating scene and I haven't allowed myself to get too involved with anyone else since.

After our steamy encounter in the conference room, I certainly want to get more involved with my masked man. Again, it's so unlike me to do something like this. But maybe it's a good thing, and exactly what I need in my life. Going out on a limb, taking a chance and meeting someone…I need to throw caution to the wind and jump into the deep end. No more holding back and no more fear.

Vowing to grab this opportunity, to seize it without any second-guessing, I shove any lingering doubts aside and decide to take the biggest chance of my life.

I'm going to open myself up to a man without regard to the possible repercussions. Hopefully, he reciprocates and this will be the beginning of something wonderful.

If not, well, it'll mean another heartbreak for me.

Be positive, I tell myself, shaking off the perpetual doubts that always seem to plague me.

It's almost time now and my belly flutters with excited nerves. Or, maybe that's the lingering ripples from the incredible orgasm he gave me.

I'm so wrapped up in my thoughts, I don't notice the two large shadows that appear from the rear edge of the garden. Not until they're practically upon me. Without warning, two masked men appear on either side of me and scare the crap out of me. I tell myself to relax—this is a masquerade party, after all—and decide to move around to the other side of the fountain.

Before I can do that, though, firm hands grab each of my elbows and turn me toward the back section where a gate leads out to the alley. Shocked, I try to break free and attempt to scream, but my cries are smothered when a big, meaty hand slaps over my mouth.

"Keep quiet or I'll hurt you," the man in the jester mask threatens, his voice low and scary.

The other man wears a ghost mask and yanks me along, his grip punishing. I struggle, trying to twist away, doing anything to break their steel grips, but it's useless.

Fear pummels through me as they whisk me through the courtyard, away from the hotel and the crowd of party goers, and straight to a waiting SUV with black-tinted windows. Heart in my throat, I struggle harder and try to cry out for help, but they're too strong and fast.

As one of the men opens the rear door, I try to twist away and cry out, "No! Please!"

Before I realize it, they toss me into the backseat and the locks click. My eyes go wide as I sit up and do my best not to completely panic. Who are these men? What is going on? Why do they want me?

I have no idea what the hell is going on or why I've been abducted. And I have a feeling they aren't going to answer any of my questions. Even so, I try to get some answers. I also take comfort in the fact that I have my cell phone tucked away in my wristlet. Slipping a hand into my small red and black purse, I wrap my fingers around my phone and slowly pull it out.

"Where are we going?" I ask. My attention drops to the screen and I pull up Miceli's name.

I'm in a black SUV, I text him. *Two men dragged me away from the party. No idea where they're taking me...I'm scared.*

My finger punches send and I discreetly slip the phone back into my wristlet. Even though I'm frightened, I'm also angry. These assholes just forced me to leave the party before I was able to meet with my mystery man who I can't stop thinking about.

"Where?" I demand, untying my mask and hiding it in the folds of my voluminous skirt. Jester glances over his shoulder and glares at me.

"Shut up," he snaps. "You'll find out soon enough."

I clamp my mouth shut and turn my attention out the window, watching the passing scenery, trying to get a fix on my location and, more importantly, my destination. Hopefully, I can get another text sent off to Miceli.

Speaking of which, my phone buzzes and Jester's head snaps back around.

"What was that?"

Oh, shit. God, he must have supersonic hearing or something.

He turns all the way around, zeroing in on the wristlet tucked beneath my dress. "Bitch has a phone," he snarls then reaches over the seat and rips my wristlet away. Horror fills me when he rolls down the window and throws it out onto the street.

My heart sinks. *Shit, shit, shit.* I'm wondering what Miceli texted and now I'm starting to panic. I'm not used to danger or any kind of excitement. My brothers and their significant others are the ones who experience love and adventure, not me. My life is boring, predictable and definitely not romantic in any sort of way.

But, there's no denying I'm in serious trouble right now. The more I think about it, the more scared I get. I have no idea what's happening and no one who could potentially save me has any idea where these thugs are taking me—myself included.

So how is anyone going to come to my rescue? I wonder a little desperately.

They're not, a little voice states.

I pull in a deep breath and force myself to calm down, face the situation head-on and think logically. Okay, so one thing becomes clear fast—I'm going to have to rescue myself. One way or another, I'm going to have to dig deep and be smart. There's no time to play the damsel in distress.

Channeling my inner badass, I pay close attention to my surroundings and realize we're heading into a bad part of town. There aren't many people on the streets and the ones I see look like drug addicts and vagrants. I have a feeling they have their own problems and I can't rely on them to step up and help me fight off my kidnappers. They're probably too high to help me, anyway.

Just as well, Lottie, I tell myself. *I can handle this. Somehow.*

Even though I try to remain calm, my pulse is beating so hard and fast, and I'm sweating bullets. How could things have taken such a drastic turn in such a short amount of time? One second I'm kissing my hot masked man and now I'm being spirited away by a couple of thugs to God-knows-where.

Maybe the worst part is that I'll never figure out who he was or see him again. Because these idiots dragged me away, I'll never find my mysterious stranger and he's going to think I stood him up when I'm not at the fountain for our rendezvous. That hurts way more than it probably should.

Focus, I chastise myself.

Now isn't the time to think about what could've been. Now is the time to step up and escape. I can have a pity party later.

Eventually, the SUV pulls up in front of a rundown house. After parking at the curb, Jester and Ghost get out, walk over and open my door.

"Out," Jester snaps, and I glare at him as I slide out of the car.

He grabs my upper arm, turns me toward the rundown house and begins tugging me up the uneven walkway. It's made up of broken concrete with weeds sprouting up through the cracks, a total tripping hazard. Halfway to the house, I nonchalantly drop my mask still hidden in my voluminous skirts and send up a silent prayer.

If my brothers can somehow figure out where I am then maybe they'll see my mask laying on the sidewalk. It's probably a longshot, but there's always the possibility. And right now, I need some luck on my side and to remain positive.

The house is dark and dirty-looking with several boarded-up windows. It's clearly abandoned, maybe even a drug house, and I squint against the gloominess, my eyes slowly adjusting. We walk inside and a musty smell hangs in the air and I wrinkle my nose. I also catch the unpleasant scent of something that's been decaying for a while. Probably a mouse or rat lost in the walls or under the slanted floorboards.

The thugs cart me into a side room on the first floor and Ghost shoves me down into a wooden chair. Jester binds my hands to the chair's arms with zip ties and I try not to let panic consume me. Forcing myself to remain cool and in control, ready to seize any opportunity to escape that might prevent itself, I focus on calming and slowing my breathing.

"I'll let Gallo know we're here," Ghostface says and walks out.

My heart falls. I should've known Carmine Gallo was behind this, but I didn't connect the dots. Miceli and my brothers had warned us all about Gallo, and after Angelo and Blake's dealings with the man and his mansion burning down, I should've been more alert. More careful.

But, no, I was too consumed by lust for a man whose name I don't even know and will never see again.

So stupid, Lottie, I scold myself, pulling against the zip ties. I was so eager to fall in love that I wasn't paying enough attention to my surroundings. To be fair, though, I hardly expected to be abducted from the hotel when there were so many people around.

Not outside, though, I remind myself. For the briefest moment, I wonder if the masked stranger was a part of my abduction. Did he purposely lure me outside and away from the rest of the guests? I suppose it's a possibility, bt=ut one that I don't want to think about too hard. Because I briefly allowed myself to trust a man again—and if he is the reason for my current situation, I don't think I'll ever be able to trust anyone ever again.

"Well, well, well, if it isn't Carlotta Rossi," Gallo says, walking into the room. He looks so damn smug that I want to punch him.

"Are you crazy? You can't just kidnap me!" I exclaim.

"Really? Because I think I just did," he states arrogantly.

He comes right up to me, grabs my chin and snaps it up, forcing me to look into his fleshy face, twisted in anger. Gritting my teeth, I return his stare with all of the defiance I can muster, but cold fear trickles through my veins. He has a crazed, wide-eyed look that makes me shiver.

"You better shake, Carlotta, because I have plans for you. Plans you will not like, but things that must be done to teach your family a lesson."

"My family didn't do anything to you," I tell him.

"So naive. You have no idea what you're talking about. They're the reason I haven't been invited to join the other mafia families, they're the reason I was put on the Kill List and hunted down by crazed bounty hunters and they're the reason my mansion burned to the ground. I will have my revenge," he seethes.

I squirm in the chair and he snaps my face to the side.

"I'm going to destroy your family…starting with you."

Oh, God. I do my best not to show fear, but it's getting harder and harder. Miceli knows I'm in trouble, but how will he find me? That asshole tossed my phone out the car window.

Gallo is deranged. I need to escape fast and I know time is of the essence.

But how?

You're on your own, Lottie. Time to figure it out.

6

ARCHER

The water flows softly in the fountain beside me and I look down at the two glasses of champagne I'm holding and frown. *God, I'm a sucker.* Setting them down on a nearby side table a little too hard, the glass clinks.

I'm annoyed as I turn around and look back toward the party. Is she still in there? Maybe out on the dance floor with a new partner? Clearly, making it out here to meet me wasn't a priority for her. I certainly arrived in a timely fashion and more eager than a fucking schoolboy.

So pathetic.

Is she with someone else?

A strange wave of possessiveness washes over me and I'm not used to feeling like this. In fact, I don't like it at all. The urge to storm back inside and hunt her down fills me and I take a step toward the door when a sound snags my attention. Almost like a scuffling sound.

"No! Please!" a woman cries out.

Spinning around, I squint through the trees and see a flash of red and white. Without a doubt, I know it's my Queen of Hearts…and I have a sinking feeling she's in trouble. I take off running, yanking my mask off and tossing it as I race toward the back of the property. After pushing through the rear gate, I wind up in the alley just in time to see the object of my desire get roughly shoved into a black SUV.

Shocked, I take a moment to assess the situation as the car takes off, fleeing into the night. In a split second, I make the decision to go after them. Even though I don't know who she is or what kind of trouble she might be in, I'm going to find out.

I didn't leave my car with the valet because I don't trust anyone and I don't like waiting around, especially if I need to make a quick getaway. Like now. Therefore, my black Dodge Challenger is parked very close by and I race across the street, hop inside and turn it on. The engine roars to life and I shove it into gear. Smoke pours from the tires as I yank the wheel hard and slam on the gas.

Here we go.

There's no way I'm letting them get away from me and I peel around the corner at the end of the alley. Traffic is busy enough that it'll slow the other car down, but not too much that we'll be sitting in it and crawling along. After a minute of driving like a maniac, way too fast, weaving in and out of other cars, I see the SUV.

I fall in behind another car, staying close, but not obviously close. The neighborhoods seem to be getting worse and worse as we drive further into the city. At some point, something gets thrown out the SUV's window and I think it might be the little purse my girl was carrying.

It doesn't take a genius to realize the bastards tossed her phone and identification. And that doesn't bode well.

My blood starts pumping harder and anger courses through me. I know she's in trouble, but why? Everything in me shifts into protector mode and I refuse to let anything bad happen to her.

Dammit, I wish I knew her name, knew her story.

The idea that she'd already been outside waiting for me makes my heart soar. She didn't stand me up, after all. No, my little brunette was already out there by the fountain waiting, eager to see me again. But then a couple of assholes dragged her away and ruined all of my plans.

The question is why? What's going on?

Determined to get to the bottom of the situation, I accelerate, making sure I don't lose my quarry. After a little more driving, the SUV pulls up alongside the curb in a shitty neighborhood. I drive past and turn the corner at the end of the block. Once I'm out of sight, I park the car and reach over and open the glove box. Reaching inside, I pull out my Glock 19. Never leave home without it—and it's a good thing, too. I get out, lock my car and jog back to the end of the block, using houses and shrubs for cover.

My attention zeroes in on my girl being forcefully escorted up a walkway and straight into a dilapidated house. Her mask is off and she's even more beautiful than I imagined. I don't miss it when she drops her red mask on the sidewalk. *Smart little thing.* She's leaving a clue, a breadcrumb, a cry for help.

I don't know who she is, but I know she's in trouble and I'm about to knock some thugs out and rescue her. Because, hey, it's what I'm good at—taking down the bad guys.

Once they're out of sight, I hurry across the neighboring lawns then head for the backyard. I'm going to break in through the back door. But first, I sneak up to a grimy-looking window and peer through the dirty glass.

I see the trio move through the living room and disappear into another room on the opposite side of the house. A plan starts forming in my head as I make my way in a low crouch toward the rear of the property. Even though I only saw two thugs, it doesn't mean there isn't another tango in there who I'll need to take down.

Guard up, gun in hand, I step onto the rickety back porch and stealthily make my way to the back door. I try turning the knob and it surprisingly opens. *Hmmm.* Not sure if that's good or bad, but I push it open and slip inside.

Voices waft out from the room on the left and I creep forward, listening to the conversation, catching bits and pieces. When I'm right outside the door, I can hear more clearly and, for a stunned moment, I freeze.

"You better shake, Carlotta, because I have plans for you. Plans you will not like, but things that must be done to teach your family a lesson."

Carlotta? As in Carlotta *Rossi*?

Oh, fuck…fuck me for so many different reasons.

"My family didn't do anything to you," she says, doing her best to sound brave.

I dare to look into the room, through the cracked door, and I see Carlotta sitting in a chair, wrists zip tied to its armrests. Carmine fucking Gallo stands in front of her, spouting off his threats, and the two thugs stand off to the side, both armed.

"You have no idea what you're talking about," Gallo states coldly. "They're the reason I haven't been invited to join the other mafia families, they're the reason I was put on the Kill List and hunted down by crazed bounty hunters and they're the reason my mansion burned to the ground. I will have my revenge."

God, what a fucking crybaby. I'm looking forward to hurting him.

"I'm going to destroy your family…starting with you," Gallo seethes.

That's it. I've had enough. Moving faster than those two slightly-overweight thugs can handle, I sweep into the room, staying low and fast, and fire off a round into each goon. They drop before they even know what the hell hit them.

Meanwhile, Gallo dives for cover and crawls away fast, disappearing into an adjoining room. I have the briefest opportunity to shoot him in the ass, but I turn to Carlotta instead.

"Are you okay?" I ask, looking her over quickly. She doesn't seem hurt and relief fills me.

She stares at me, mouth dropping open, and blinks. "You're…from the party," she finishes lamely because she still has no idea who I am.

I nod then decide I should get Gallo. "Hang on, sweetheart."

Storming into the attached room, expecting a bathroom, I realize it's exactly that. Except, it connects to an adjoining room and Gallo must've fled through it and escaped. I make sure, though, and follow through. The back door now stands wide open, confirming my suspicion.

It doesn't matter. I'll let Miceli know and someone will take care of Gallo very soon. That asshole just signed his own death warrant by crossing the Rossi family yet again.

Once I do a more thorough sweep and make sure he really is gone, I return to Carlotta. I slip my pistol in my back waistband then pull out the Ka-Bar tucked into a sheath in my boot.

"Hold still," I murmur and slice through the zip ties, freeing her dainty wrists. She's looking up at me like I'm some kind of famous actor and she's starstruck. I can see the little hearts floating in her eyes as I offer her my hand.

"We need to go," I say, and she immediately tucks her small hand in mine. The fact that she trusts me makes me puff my chest out a little.

"Who are you?" she whispers.

But I don't answer, just pull her through the house and out the front door.

"C'mon, I'm parked down here," I tell her. Once we reach my Challenger, I unlock it and open the passenger door for her. "Get in and let's call your brother."

After she slips inside, I close the door and circle around. Once I'm in the driver's seat, I pull my phone out. She reaches over and lays a hand on my arm.

"Who are you?" she asks again.

"Archer," I tell her. Recognition flares in her eyes even though we only just met tonight. She must've heard my name before, probably from Miceli.

"Oh," she breathes.

While she lets my revelation sink in, I pull up Miceli's number and hit send, making sure he's on speaker so Carlotta can hear the discussion, too.

"Rossi," he immediately answers.

"I just rescued your sister from Gallo," I say then launch into the story of what happened. Well, the part about her abduction from the masquerade party, not about how I made her orgasm with my fingers.

Miceli is pissed as hell, just like I knew he would be, and Carlotta assures him that she's okay.

"Gallo said he's going to destroy our family, Miceli," Carlotta tells him, leaning forward, hands twisting in her skirts. "I'm not sure what he would've actually done to me—"

"He was going to kill you," I interrupt, being blunt, and needing them both to understand the seriousness of the situation. "Don't delude yourself into thinking otherwise or doubt him. I heard the anger in his voice. He's not fucking around and both of his men were armed. I think Carlotta needs to be taken somewhere safe."

I glance over at her and the look on her face is completely unreadable.

"Do you have a place?" Miceli asks.

"Yeah. Somewhere off the grid that no one knows about."

"Okay, take her there and I'm going to talk to Gallo."

Talk or take care of him? I wonder. But I don't ask. I'm not sure how much Carlotta knows about what her older brother has done—the lengths to which he's gone to protect the people he loves. I have a feeling, though, the time is coming soon where she's going to have her rose-tinted glasses ripped off. Whether she likes it or not.

Because we aren't a good group of men. Miceli and his brothers will do whatever it takes to protect the people they care about and it doesn't matter how many dead bodies turn up in order to do that. And I'm the guy who will help them take care of business.

In fact, I'll kill whoever I need to if the payment or the motivation is right. I lost my conscience a long time ago.

After so many years on a ghost ops teams doing secret, deadly missions, pulling a trigger and neutralizing tangoes doesn't affect me anymore. I figure I'm doing the world a favor by eliminating scum, dirt bags and bad guys.

"Do I get a say in any of this?" Carlotta asks.

"No," Miceli and I respond at the same time.

She lets out a frustrated huff then coolly reminds us she has no clothes and is wearing a ballgown.

"I have stuff," I say, my voice gruff. Although, my dirty mind is already picturing what perky assets might be hidden under that dress and wishing she could just be naked.

"Yeah, but I want my stuff," she insists.

"Lottie, please go with Archer. He'll keep you safe and under the radar while I deal with Gallo. It'll only be for a couple of days. Three tops. Can you do that for me?"

Carlotta sighs. "Yes," she finally agrees, and I frown.

What's the big deal? A few days off the beaten path with me isn't going to kill her. Besides, I thought she liked me. Well, I guess she did before she knew my identity.

After assuring Miceli I'll keep her safe and secure in a remote location, I disconnect the call and start the car. I have a cabin in upstate New York that will be perfect to hunker down at for a bit. It's nothing fancy, just an old hunting cabin surrounded by woods, but she doesn't need the Ritz-Carlton. Just a quiet place to hang out, far away from the dangers of New York City and Carmine Gallo.

Tightening my hands on the steering wheel, I turn toward the highway, trying not to breathe in her sweet candy smell. Because now that I know who she is—Carlotta Rossi—I know that she's off-limits.

I just hope my dick understands that he will be staying in my pants.

7

CARLOTTA

I turn in my seat and study Archer's ridiculously handsome profile intently now that the mask is long gone.

Archer.

God, never in a million years would I have guessed that the man I had a steamy make out session with at the party was my brother's elusive contact. From what I've heard Miceli say, Archer is like a ghost and most likely former military. But he doesn't know anything for sure. Not even the man's full name.

"So you're the mysterious Archer..." I murmur thoughtfully. "Is that even your real name?"

"Sure," he responds vaguely.

I let out a snort of disbelief. "That doesn't sound very convincing."

"I can be whoever you want me to be, Carlotta," he states smoothly and turns the car onto the freeway.

"How do you know my brother?"

"I know all your brothers."

He's so evasive and I cross my arms. "Where exactly are we going?"

"Upstate."

Frustration fills me. He's answering my questions, but at the same time, he's not giving me any new information. For the next ten minutes, he focuses on driving and I chew my lower lip until it starts bleeding. *Dammit.*

I can feel him pulling away, closing off to me. And that's the last thing I want because I'm so attracted to him. We were hot and heavy, but now he's cool as a cucumber. And I know exactly why.

It's because I'm Miceli Rossi's little sister.

"Why does it matter that I'm Miceli's sister?" I ask, going for bluntness and laying my cards out on the table. Because the man sitting beside me is nothing like the one I met at the masquerade party. My steamy stranger is now a distant memory. In his place is a man who won't even talk to me much less look in my direction.

For a long moment he doesn't say anything. Just sort of mulls over my question. Then he sends me a quick side glance and says, "It matters a lot."

"But why?" I press, not letting him off the hook so easily.

"It's not a line I want to cross."

"Don't you think we already crossed that line?"

"Not the most important one. No."

My face screws up in a frown. He's basically telling me he regrets what we did and now he won't touch me with a ten foot pole. *Thanks a lot, Miceli.* God, talk about clitorference. Why is everyone so damn scared of Big, Bad Miceli Rossi? I mean, yes, he's huge and intimidating, but Archer is no slouch. He's got a dark intimidation factor working in his favor, too. Not to mention he's well over six feet and solid muscle. I suppose he's built more slimly than my brother, but still very athletic.

"Are you scared of my brother?" I ask, crossing my arms, getting straight to the point.

"I'm not scared of anyone," he says without hesitation.

Then the worst possible thought enters my head. Maybe after he saw me without the mask on, he's no longer attracted to me. I rub a hand over my heart and the urge to cry hits me. Is that why he's being so cool now? He just doesn't think I'm pretty and it's as simple as that.

Suddenly, I'm so embarrassed and I don't want to even look at him. Turning the other way, I face the window and stare out at the passing night and cars. Rejection hurts and I know that better than anyone. The only guy I ever dated rejected me and slept with another woman right before I almost slept with him. It was humiliating.

Painful memories of Rendall and what a fiasco that relationship was—if you could even call it that—fill me and my heart aches. What is wrong with me? Am I that undesirable? It seemed like Archer wanted me, but that's when he didn't know who I was and maybe it was just exciting because we were strangers wearing masks.

I really have no idea. A part of me wants to ask him. But there's no way in hell I'm going to subject myself to further embarrassment. No, thank you. I've experienced enough mortification for the night.

Since I don't say anything to keep the conversation going, the rest of the drive is absolutely silent. At some point, I close my eyes, lean my head against the window, and drift in and out of a light sleep.

I'm not sure how much time passes when I hear the crunching of gravel beneath the tires and open my eyes. A quick glance at the glowing numerals on the dashboard tells me it's been a couple of hours and I yawn, sitting up and leaning forward to get a better look out the windshield.

It's pitch black out and we're really in the middle of nowhere. Tall trees surround us and after driving down a long, winding driveway, a small cabin comes into view.

"Where are we?" I ask sleepily. My dress feels too tight and all I want to do is take it off and slip into a warm, comfy bed.

"My place. It's safe," he assures me.

"Sorry for being such an inconvenience."

"It's fine."

"I didn't mean to ruin your evening."

Archer stops the car in front of the cabin and looks over at me. "Ruin my evening?" he echoes, a dark brow arching. "Sweetheart, you were the best part of tonight."

My heart flutters in my chest and he's looking at me so intently that I can't even string a sentence together.

"C'mon, let's go inside," he says and gets out.

I open my door and a cold breeze whips my hair and skirt up, chilling me. Rubbing my hands up and down my bare arms, I watch him open the trunk and pull out a duffel bag.

"Wow. You're prepared," I comment. Why does he have a packed bag with him? "Were you planning on coming up here after the party?"

But he shakes his head. "No. I just always have a bag ready."

"Why?"

"In case I need to leave fast." He eyes me. "Why do you ask so many questions?"

"I'm inquisitive," I tell him with a cheeky grin.

"Clearly." His tone is dry, but he gives me the hint of a smile. "Let's go inside before you freeze. I have some clothes you can borrow so you can get out of that dress."

"Oh, thank you," I gush, following him up the steps and waiting while he unlocks the door. "I can't wait to get this thing off. As pretty as it is, I'd like nothing more than a pair of comfy seats and a T-shirt."

"That can be arranged."

We go inside and Archer flips on a light then locks the door behind us. There's a chill in the air and he turns the heat on as I move forward, looking around. It's small, but oh-so charming. A large fireplace takes up one wall with a worn, comfy-looking couch in front of it. There's a small kitchenette and stairs that go up to a loft which I assume is a bedroom. It seems like he hasn't been here in a while because I notice a light coating of dust on the entryway table.

"This is nice," I say, clasping my hands in front of me and rubbing them briskly.

"I can make a fire," he tells me, noticing that I'm cold. "Fair warning, it'll heat this place up fast."

"I won't say no to a nice, warm fire." I watch him lean over, unzip the duffel bag and start digging around inside. His tight ass pops out from under his suit jacket, giving me quite the view and I lick my lips.

"Sweetheart, you were the best part of tonight."

His words repeat over and over in my head, making me wonder if he actually is interested. He must be, right? Why else would he have said such a thing?

Archer stands back up and turns around. Of course, he catches me staring at his delicious ass which turns into his crotch because he's now facing me. And, oh my, is there a lot to look at. My face flushes and I force my eyes up, meeting his which look even darker than before. Something flashes through his espresso gaze, but I'm not sure what.

Desire maybe?

He clears his throat, holding out a shirt and sweatpants.

"Thanks," I mumble, taking them.

"Go ahead and use the bathroom first while I get a fire going. You can have the bed up in the loft."

"Where will you sleep?" I ask, feeling bad if there's only one bed.

"On the couch."

"I can sleep on the c—"

"It's fine." I give him a doubtful look. He has ridiculously long legs that are going to hang right off the edge. "Really, I don't mind."

"Only if you're sure," I insist.

"I'm sure. Now go wash up. It's late."

He's right and I'm exhausted. Turning on my heel, I head over to what I assume is the bathroom and step inside. Like the rest of the cabin, it's small, nothing elaborate, until I see the shower.

"Oh, wow." I walk over and check it out. There's no door and it's wide-open with a smooth stone wall and a big, waterfall shower head above. "Very fancy."

I'm too tired to use it now, but I will definitely try it out tomorrow. Right now, I just want to change. After kicking off my heels, I reach around and attempt to unzip myself. It doesn't go so well. After struggling for a few minutes, I let out a soft curse.

This dress isn't coming off without some help.

Mustering up my courage, I open the bathroom door and look out to see Archer bent over again, lighting the kindling. Damn, that ass of his is a sight to behold.

"Um, Archer?"

His head snaps around. "Yes?"

"Can you, ah, help me?"

He immediately stands up, brushing his hands off on his suit pants, and walking over. "Sure. What do you need? There should be a new toothbrush in the cabinet."

"Actually, I need you to unzip me."

His eyes roam hungrily down my body and heat seems to flare within their dark depths. Unless it's just my overactive imagination, he looks very, very interested.

"Oh, right." He gives me a nod and motions for me to spin around.

I turn around, presenting him with my back and he grabs the zipper and slowly tugs it downward. And something inside me lights up. His warm, slightly rough knuckles touch my skin and it's like a light caress trailing down my back. A shiver runs through my body and I squeeze my eyes shut, pressing my thighs together.

Good Lord, this man has the power to wreck me. All sorts of wicked thoughts begin to fill my head. Like what would it be like to have Archer as my first lover.

"Done." His voice sounds raspier than usual and a slow, steady throbbing makes my pussy pulse.

Swallowing hard, I turn back around, clutching the dress to my chest so it doesn't fall open and give him a show. Even though I am slightly tempted to let it slide down a little. Maybe give him a peek.

"Thank you," I murmur. He gives me a sharp nod then turns and walks out. With a soft sigh, I sag against the edge of the counter.

My thoughts whirl as I find the new toothbrush along with some toothpaste. Archer is the most delicious man I've ever laid eyes on and I'm debating over what to do about the situation.

After brushing my teeth, I find a facewash and I scrub all my makeup off. It belatedly occurs to me how different I probably look because I went all out tonight with smoky eyes, sparkles and red lips. Now, I look at myself in the mirror and feel like I just washed most of my self-confidence down the drain.

What if Archer doesn't find me attractive anymore? I also look a lot younger than I did with a clean, fresh face. Oh, well. There's not much I can do about it now. But one thing has firmly taken root in my mind —I am stuck in this cabin for the next few days with the hottest man I've ever encountered who is giving me more than just a few butterflies. More like a million.

The timing feels right to spice things up. And, honestly, what have I got to lose? Other than my virginity? My life has been boring and predictable for so long, and Archer excites me in a way Rendall never did.

Of course, he might not be interested. That would be tragic and would no doubt shatter my ego. But, it's a chance I'm willing to take. Mustering up all of my courage, I make a decision: I'm going to seduce Archer.

8

ARCHER

The fire crackles loudly, pouring off heat, and it's not long before the main room is toasty warm. I can't stop thinking about unzipping Carlotta's dress and how soft her skin felt against my knuckles. The temptation to do more was almost my undoing. But, I held it together and didn't rip the dress off like I so desperately wanted to do.

She is Miceli's baby sister, I remind myself sternly. For fuck's sake, the man would have my balls ripped off and shoved down my throat for doing half the things that have gone through my mind. Dirty things that would make her scream in pleasure and end with us both coming so damn hard.

No! Forget about it.

Christ, I'm starting to sweat it's so damn hot in here already. Tossing my suit jacket, I yank my tie off, unbutton my sleeves and roll them up, exposing the crossed arrows inked on my left forearm. My ghost ops team all got the same tattoo. It's where our nicknames came from —there was Arrow, Bow, Fletch, Bolt, Pierce and me, Archer. Our team's name was Sagittarius and we specialized in killing the enemy silently. As if we were a bow and arrow, we'd slice through the night, find our target and take them down swiftly.

Those days seem so long ago and I miss those guys. But after we parted ways, they met women, started families and began truly living their lives. While I, on the other hand, stayed in the shadows.

"It's so warm."

I glance up and see the object of my lusty desire walk back into the living room. She carefully lays her dress over a chair and now wears my T-shirt and jogging pants. And, fuck me, she barely looks twenty years old. The makeup is gone, all washed away, and she's so fresh-faced and exuding such a beautiful youthfulness, it makes my chest and groin tighten simultaneously.

"Too warm?" I ask, forcing my attention to the fire now raging. Just like my out of control hormones. "I can take a log off."

"No, it feels wonderful. I'm just surprised how quickly it warmed up."

She moves closer and I swallow hard. My body is already reacting to her, wanting her, and this isn't good. But, she's utterly stunning and I'm just a man. One who hasn't had sex in a while. It's a combustible situation and I feel like the fire and she's hot, dry tinder. And, goddamn, I want to light her up in every possible way.

Clamping my jaw, I grind my teeth together and try to ignore the growing heaviness in my pants. "I'm sure you're tired," I force out. "The bed is up in the loft. So…goodnight."

I know it's a brush-off, but I'm not sure how much more I can take. So, yes, please go up there so I can disappear into the bathroom and jerk off. But, instead of heading up to the loft, she moves closer to me. Her sweet candy scent infiltrates my senses and I curl my hands into fists.

"Archer," she says softly, shyly, "I don't mind if you join me."

What? My eyes lock onto hers and she's right in front of me now, her gaze drifting down my body like a caress, and it's almost more than I can take. I'm remembering how her lips tasted, how eagerly she kissed me back when I had her up on that conference room table. How good it felt to grind against her wet panties then sink my fingers in her hot, slick pussy.

On the verge of overheating, I throw all common sense out the window, grab her wrist and yank her against my hard, desperate body. My mouth crashes into hers, needy and demanding, and I force my tongue past her lips. She's so damn eager, her tongue meeting and dueling with mine, pushing up onto her toes and giving as good as she's getting. Of course, her excitement gets me even more revved up and I walk her backwards toward the couch.

I can't think straight when it comes to this woman. At least my brain can't and it lets my dick take over. Big mistake, but I'm a goner, lost in sensation. It's crazy, and before I can comprehend what's happening, I have her down on the couch and I lower myself on top of her, kissing her sweet mouth as though my very life depended on it. Kissing my Queen of Hearts into sweet, fucking oblivion.

Deepening the kiss, I feel her wrap her legs around my waist, drawing me right where she wants me. Slowly, seductively, she rubs her hot center against my hard dick and I groan into her mouth.

"You're driving me crazy," I growl, thrusting against her needy pussy, unable to forget how wet she got for me earlier. So tight, so drenched, so responsive.

"I wasn't sure you liked me," she murmurs, circling her hips harder and breathing faster.

I lift my head so I can look down at her, look right into her pretty brown eyes. And I hate the doubt I see there. "Are you kidding me?" I rasp. "I wanted to fuck you since the moment I laid eyes on you at the dessert table."

She blinks, mouth opening slightly, as though not quite sure she heard me right. "Really?"

"Sweetheart, I want you so badly it hurts," I admit.

"Then take me," she says, arching beneath me, offering herself up.

The reality of our situation makes me stop the descent of my hand which was headed down to cup one of her luscious breasts. I've been entrusted to care for her and protect her, not take advantage of her. It feels like someone just dumped a bucket of ice water over my head and I force myself to pull back. To rein my lust in and get myself in check. Everything in me rebels, but I know I don't have a choice in the matter.

Carlotta Rossi isn't mine to take and even though I'd like nothing more than to enjoy this sweet body of hers, I can't.

"Fuck," I hiss and pull away. I'm not sure where this sudden crisis of conscience is coming from. Or, maybe it's just the uncomfortable thought of Miceli killing me. I roll off her, stand up and rake a frustrated hand through my hair.

"Archer?"

Squeezing my eyes shut, I do the only thing I can—push her away. "Go to bed, Carlotta."

I hear her sit up, but I don't dare turn around with the massive erection I'm sporting.

"Did I…do something wrong?" she asks, voice laced in doubt.

I hate how timid she sounds now and I mentally berate myself. "I need to text your brother. Go up to the loft. Now," I grit out far more harshly than I intend.

I hear her scramble up off the couch and see her head up the steps from the corner of my eye. Battling my lust and loyalty, I turn and stalk into the bathroom, slamming the door shut behind me.

Throwing my clothes off, I turn the shower on, step beneath the falling water and grasp my stiff cock.

Yeah, it would've been much better finding relief inside Carlotta's soft, willing body, but that would be crossing a line that I'm not yet willing to cross. Realistically, I can't say I won't eventually. Never say never, right? Right now, however, I'm going to keep my distance, relieve this ache then let Miceli know we're safe.

Well, I'm not sure how safe Carlotta is from my dirty thoughts but, for the moment, no one is going to hurt her. I'll make damn sure of that. Not on my watch.

Standing beneath the spray, I pump my steel length until I erupt, shooting thick ropes of semen against the tiled wall. Groaning through my release, I drop my head against the cool tile and wonder how much longer I can avoid fucking Carlotta. She's far too tempting.

Sure, I was a gentleman tonight. Well, as much of a gentleman as I can be. I restrained myself from taking what she freely offered. But if she does it again, I'm not going to be able to say no.

And here's the thing. I don't do relationships after what happened with Caitlin. So where does that leave me and Carlotta? It leaves us in one-night stand territory. Or two nights, more than likely…and that's not something that can happen. Well, it can, but it shouldn't. If I have one shred of decency left, I should respect Miceli's baby sister, right?

I'm not a good guy, though. Never have been, never will be. And that puts me in quite the predicament.

After finding a semblance of relief, I get out of the shower, towel off and pull on a pair of flannel pajama bottoms. Although I much rather sleep in my boxer briefs or nothing at all, I put the bottoms on because the last thing I want is to run into Carlotta and be naked. That wouldn't end well.

Technically, it would end up with us probably having sex on the floor. Or up against the wall. Or, maybe on the table.

"Christ," I hiss and shove a hand through my wet hair. Why the hell did I tell Miceli I could bring Carlotta up here and keep her safe for a few days? Because the truth is, she isn't safe with me. Not at all.

Despite that fact, I wander back into the living and look up to the loft. It's dark and quiet, so I assume she's in bed. My bed. And she's leaving her cotton candy scent all over my sheets. Fucking torture.

Yeah, it's really important that I stay down here where I can't touch her or smell her or reach for her.

Grabbing my phone, I pull up Miceli's name and shoot off a short text, letting him know we're here and we're safe. He really doesn't need to know I'm a second away from seducing his little sister.

After I hit send, I set my phone on the coffee table and stretch out on the couch. My legs hang over the edge, but it's not too uncomfortable. It's so warm right here in front of the fireplace that I don't even need the blanket laying on the back of the couch. Besides, I'm still too hot for Carlotta.

With one hand tucked behind my head and the other resting on my chest, I think over the last few hours. Damn, I wish my Queen of Hearts hadn't turned out to be a Rossi. It's not that I'm scared of them or anything, but Miceli and his brothers and I have a relationship that I don't want to screw up. Because if I screwed Carlotta, everything would go to hell fast.

And I wouldn't blame them for getting pissed at me.

I know I can be a dick and when it's time to be ruthless, I have no problem doing it. But, as a general rule, I don't like to lead women on or hurt them. The simple truth is I tried a relationship once and it ended in more than just disaster. It ended in her dying.

Who I am, what I do…it's fucking dangerous. Always has been. So the best thing I can do is stay far away from Carlotta Rossi. It's going to be hard, but it's for the best. When I hook up with a woman, she needs to understand all I can give of myself is one night. It'll be a damn good time, but I'm not going to hang around for anything long term. I always make that crystal clear and certain women also enjoy that kind of relationship. One where pleasure is exchanged and then we both go on our merry way.

But Carlotta is a whole different breed of woman. She's a lady and deserves to be treated as such.

With a curse, I punch a fist into my pillow, turn onto my side then lay my head back down and stare into the flames. I wish things could be different, but they aren't. Except…

There's one scenario that might make me change my mind about sleeping with Carlotta. If she would agree to only one night and she fully understood the rules and ramifications then things might be different. I'd need us both to be on exactly the same page and have the same expectations. Plus, we'd need to keep it a secret.

One glorious night of fucking each other's brains out. Then we go our separate ways once we return to the city.

I suppose it's possible, but I'm certainly not going to suggest a one-night stand no matter how epic I know it would be. However, if she brings it up and agrees to my stipulations then there's no way in hell I'd be able to resist.

Ball's in her court, I think, my eyes growing heavy, the crackling fire lulling me to sleep.

And the asshole part of me is really hoping she tries to seduce me again.

9

CARLOTTA

Sleeping alone in Archer's bed, I turn onto my back and sigh. After thinking everything over and picking it all apart, I come to one conclusion: Archer likes kissing and touching me, but he doesn't like that I'm a Rossi. For whatever reason, he's putting his loyalty to my brothers first, over his desire for me. It's the only explanation for why he keeps pulling away since he discovered my true identity.

And that isn't acceptable.

Somehow, I'm going to convince him to give me a chance and let go of whatever is holding him back. It's not fair or right that my brothers dictate my love life. I am a grown-ass woman and should be allowed to sleep with whomever I choose. They sure always have done whatever they want when it comes to the opposite sex.

A part of me feels rejected, though, and it's a horrible feeling. But I truly believe Archer is only hesitant because our family is powerful and intimidating. I refuse to give up so soon because I'm pretty certain he likes me. And this man interests me on every level and all I want to do is get to know him better. So that's my plan. For the next few days I'm going to smother him with charm and as much sex appeal as I can muster. I plan to use every tool in my arsenal to wear him down.

The next morning, I launch Operation: Activate Archer's Libido. I decide it's the little things that might inevitably push him over the edge—brushing past him, lightly touching him when the opportunity arises, flirting shamelessly, telling him I appreciate everything he does, letting him catch me checking him out and any other opportunity I find.

At the end of the next day, I realize he's a very stubborn man. Any time I came close or had the chance to touch him, I took it. There were so many moments that I saw heat and interest flicker in the depths of his dark eyes, but then he'd douse it so fast my head would spin.

By dinner time, I am beyond frustrated and trying to figure out what else I can do. The situation is starting to feel hopeless, but I knew it would be a challenge and I am not giving up.

There isn't a whole lot in the pantry, just some non-perishable items, so we end up making some boxed macaroni and cheese. I find a pan and put the water on to boil while Archer sets the table with bowls and silverware.

"How often do you come up here?" I ask, trying to make conversation.

"It's been a few months," he answers, plucking out two bottles of cold water from the fridge. "I like getting away from the city, but I've been busy lately."

"Busy with a girlfriend?" I keep my tone as innocent as possible, but if he tells me he has a significant other, I'm going to raise hell.

"What? No." His face screws up in a frown. I press my lips together, but don't comment further. "Just so you know, if I had a girlfriend, I wouldn't have kissed you."

"Twice," I remind him.

"Yeah. Plus I think we did a little more than kiss," he mumbles under his breath.

"At the party." I give him a wicked smile.

"I remember." Our gazes lock. "Quite clearly."

"I thought you liked me."

"I do like you." He frowns, leans a hip against the counter. "Why do you keep doubting yourself?"

"Habit." I really don't want to get into Rendall right now. I grab the box of pasta and dump it into the boiling water. Reaching for the spoon, I slowly stir it so it doesn't stick to the pan. "Am I not a good kisser?"

"What?"

I shrug a shoulder. "You haven't tried to kiss me again today, so it makes me wonder what I did wrong. Other than being a Rossi, of course," I add slyly.

A muscle flexes in his cheek.

"Because I'm thinking that's the problem," I state boldly.

"I told you, I'm not scared of your brothers. But, out of respect for them, I am going to keep my distance from you."

"Why?"

"What do you mean why?"

"If you like me and I like you then who cares what they think?"

"I care," he states stubbornly, and I make a face.

"So if I offered to get down on my knees and suck your dick right now, you'd say no? Because of my brothers?"

"Jesus, Carlotta." He shoves a hand through his thick, dark hair and looks away. But I didn't miss the flash of desire that crossed his face first. "Don't say stuff like that."

"I'm just trying to understand how my brothers figure into this. Because, Archer, I am a twenty-five year old woman who can make her own decisions. Especially when it comes to my sexual partners. Or, lack thereof," I can't help but add in a low voice.

His head snaps back over. "What do you mean 'lack thereof'? Dry spell?"

"More like the Sahara Desert," I admit.

He crosses his arm over his chest, studying me closely. "How long has it been?"

I swallow past my nerves and blurt out, "Oh, about twenty-five years."

Tilting his head as though he's not quite sure he heard me right, his mouth opens then closes. I guess words escape him and I can feel my cheeks flush with embarrassment.

"Humiliating, I know," I say, focusing on the macaroni and stirring it much too vigorously.

"Carlotta?"

I slant him a look, suddenly feeling shy. "Hmm?"

"Are you telling me you're a virgin?"

"God, don't make me say it." I roll my eyes and set the spoon down with a clink. "Yes, okay. Men avoid me like the plague. Well, except for one, but it was barely a relationship, and he just ended up breaking my heart."

I turn off the fire, take the pot over to the sink and dump the noodles in a strainer.

"What happened?" he asks quietly.

I shake the strainer, watching the steam rise, then turn and dump them back in the pot. "Cheese, please."

Archer opens the packet, moves up beside me, and sprinkles it over the hot macaroni noodles. He drops the empty envelope on the counter and he's so close, I can hear him breathing. Can feel the warmth of his body which is practically touching mine.

"What happened, sweetheart?" he asks again, his voice low.

I stir the orange powder and the noodles and let out a soft sigh. "There was a guy—Rendall—and we dated for a few months. I kept holding back, though, and couldn't fully trust him. Something didn't feel right. But, I thought maybe I was just being silly. The second I decide I'm going to sleep with him, I discover he's cheating."

"Rendall was a damn idiot."

"You can say that again."

"A total jackass."

"I broke up with him and that was that. Sahara Desert," I emphasize with a sad shake of my head.

Archer takes the pan and divides the mac and cheese into the two bowls on the table. We sit down and I scoop up a spoonful and eat it. Not the most appetizing meal, but I'm hungry and grateful there's something to eat. I can feel Archer watching me and I finally look up at him.

"What?" I ask softly.

"I'm glad you didn't sleep with that idiot."

"Rendall."

"Yeah, whatever. He didn't deserve you. And he had a stupid name"

I can't help but grin. It is a stupid name.

He swallows and takes a drink of water. "It's okay to wait, you know."

I arch a brow and make an unladylike snort. "I'm twenty-five! At this point, I'm beginning to wonder what's wrong with me."

"Absolutely nothing," he states firmly. "You're beautiful, sassy, smart… when the time is right, it'll happen."

"Easy for you to say. How many women have you slept with?"

He chokes on his food. "I'm not you."

"What's that supposed to mean?"

"I'm not looking for a relationship or a future with someone," he explains, carefully choosing his words. "My encounters are more or less relegated to one night only."

"Maybe that's all I want, too," I say stubbornly.

I can tell he doesn't believe me. And maybe it's not exactly the truth. When I see how happy my brothers are with their women, how they glow, it makes me want the same thing. Plus there's nothing sweeter than my nieces and nephews. Maybe I'm not ready for a baby tomorrow, but perhaps one day I will be. And it would be nice to have the father stick around.

"You deserve someone who will love you forever, marry you and give you babies. Not someone like me."

"FYI, Archer, I don't plan to get knocked up the first time I have sex. I want it to be a hot, unforgettable encounter with a man who knows exactly what he's doing. Someone who can teach me things and give me pleasure. Not make me an instant mom."

He swallows hard and I take a bite of food, watching him closely. A flush is creeping up his neck and he clears his throat. "It's hot in here."

He abruptly gets up and goes over to the fireplace, squats and starts fiddling around with a log. Smothering a smile, I finish my dinner and hope I made it clear I'm not looking for forever at the moment. Just a really scorching- hot right now.

A moment later he returns, finishes his dinner, and then I gather the dishes. We fall into a quiet routine where I wash them and he wipes them and puts them away.

After turning off the water, I dry my hands and say, "I'm craving something sweet. Is there anything for dessert?"

"Let me check."

Archer goes over to the pantry and takes quick inventory. "How about s'mores?" he suggests.

"Ooh, I've never had s'mores," I exclaim.

He turns back around, holding a bag of marshmallows. "Are you serious?"

"Never been camping either. I'm more of a city girl, I guess."

"Do you want to try some?"

I nod my head eagerly. "I'd love to."

He tosses me the bag of marshmallows then grabs a box of graham crackers and some chocolate. "We can do it in here since the fire is already going."

"Sounds good to me."

He grabs a couple of long sticks from a drawer and I follow him over to the fireplace where we sit down on the floor. He lays everything out on the hearth and explains how to make the perfect s'mores. He's so adorably serious and I can't help but chuckle.

"You sound like a pro," I tease. "It isn't rocket science."

"Oh, you have no idea, Ms. Rossi. If you don't get it just right then you're going to end up with a mess or have it all fall in the fire. So pay close attention and do what I do."

I can't help but smile at his boyish charm. He doesn't show it too often, but I love seeing it. After guiding me through how to assemble the perfect s'more, we hold them over the fire.

"Hold it just a little higher," he tells me, reaching for my elbow and lifting it. His warm touch sends tingles shooting up my arm.

It isn't long before the chocolate and marshmallow melt together and the graham is toasted just right. Archer checks his then motions for me to remove mine from the fire.

"All done," he tells me. "It's going to be really hot, so be careful. Let it cool."

I lightly blow on my ooey-gooey treat. We carefully remove them from the stick then I take a bite off the corner. "Ohh, it's good," I murmur. "So who taught you how to make such kick ass s'mores?"

"My dad." A sad smile lifts the edge of his mouth.

"Are the two of you close?"

"We were. He died a long time ago."

"Oh, I'm so sorry."

"Thanks. Both my parents passed away when I was only ten. A car accident."

"Oh, no. That's terrible." I can't imagine losing my mom and dad at once and being so young. I love my parents and brothers more than anything and something like that would be devastating. "Do you have any siblings?"

"No."

I shift on the floor, studying him closely, and it occurs to me that Archer is a loner. A man who has been on his own for a very long time now. No wonder he doesn't think he needs or wants a relationship.

"What happened after your parents died? Where did you go?"

"I went to live with my uncle. He wasn't very kind or warm. As soon as I turned eighteen, I enlisted. Couldn't leave fast enough. Spec ops became my life."

I get the distinct feeling he doesn't share too much of himself with other people and my heart swells. Scooting closer, I decide to be daring. I reach out and lay a hand against his stubbled cheek.

"Thank you for sharing that with me." Without thinking, I lean in and place a soft, chaste kiss on his lips. As I'm pulling back, he growls, stops me and slams his mouth against mine.

Heat floods me, arrowing south, and I try to keep up as he devours me. Kissing Archer makes me go all melty and I become more gooey than the marshmallow I just toasted. Ever since finding out my true identity, he's tried to keep his distance. But now that he's giving in, I'm going to encourage him.

Because one thing is very clear to me. Archer is unlike any man I've ever met and he is making me feel things like I've never experienced before. I want to explore whatever is happening with him and see how deep this could possibly go. If it's only one night then so be it. But if there's the possibility of having more, I'm ready to take the chance and jump in feet first.

10

ARCHER

Oh, God help me. That one innocent kiss is all it takes to make me snap. The sweet way Carlotta pressed her lips to mine, and I'm a goner. All of my self-control disappears and, as she's pulling away, I stop her, grab her face and kiss the ever-loving shit out of her.

I can't get enough and, like a man possessed, I deepen the kiss, thrusting my tongue between her soft lips. She tastes divine. Like chocolate and marshmallows, and I can't stop myself. Drinking deeply, I plunder her mouth, pushing her back onto the floor.

When she moans softly and slides her fingers through my hair, I adjust our positions, moving my knee between her legs. I know I shouldn't, but I drag her down, placing her center against my thigh and encourage her to move.

"That's it, sweetheart." I guide her hips, helping her roll and find the right spot and rhythm that gives her the best friction exactly where she wants it. "Take what you need. Rub that sweet pussy just like that."

The fact that she's a virgin and has never done this stuff with another man makes me hard as hell. Her innocence is a huge turn-on and I'm so glad that douchebag she used to date fucked it all up. She's in my arms now, riding my leg, and I'm going to make her feel so damn good. Make her realize it was worth the wait.

She's wearing my sweatpants which are way too big for her and I reach down and untie them. Her breaths are coming faster and I decide I'd rather she come on my mouth than in her panties, rubbing against my thigh. She deserves more and I'm going to make sure she gets it.

Shoving my conscience aside, ignoring that little voice telling me not to touch her and to keep my hands to myself, I tug the sweats down. Fuck that little voice. *This pussy is mine,* I think. Then I move back, taking a moment to look down and admire her. She must think that I stopped because she reaches for me with a soft sound of disappointment.

"Hold on, sweetheart. I'm going to make this even better for you."

My fingers hook in the elastic edges of her panties and I slowly pull them down to expose her sweet, pink pussy. Everything about Carlotta is delicious and I'm willing to bet she tastes just as sweet as I'm imagining. On my knees, I zero in on those pretty folds then urge her legs further apart.

"Archer," she hisses, trying to twist away.

"Hold still and open up to me, sweetheart. I'm about to lick you into an orgasm. You good with that?"

I lightly drag my thumb over her clit and she cries out, arching up.

"Yes," she whispers.

"Good." Spreading her open to me, I lean down and lick up her wet center, lapping up her juices. "Fuck, you taste good." Even better than I thought she would.

"Oh, my God," she breathes, her hands balling into fists, her hips rocking against my face.

I lick her fast then slow, gauging her reactions, trying to figure out what she likes and what gets the biggest reaction. Determined to make her feel the intensity, I languidly circle my tongue around her clit, taking my time and sucking on it until she's whimpering. Then I spear her with my tongue and rub that taut little clit until she's practically crying. The moment I slide a finger inside her, we both moan. She feels amazing—so hot and wet, tight and pulsing. I add a second finger, stretching her, making her take me all the way to my knuckles.

"Archer!"

It hits me out of nowhere that I don't want her calling me by the same name everyone else does. What we're doing…the places we're going…it's just too intimate for her to be using my call sign.

"Damon," I tell her. "Call me Damon."

Her hand slides to my head, fingers threading through my hair and pulling hard, and she looks up, locking eyes with me. "Damon," she rasps.

Hearing her say my name like that, I nearly blow. Forcing myself to maintain control, trying to ignore the throbbing erection in my pants, I focus on her and on bringing her to release. My lips wrap around her clit again and I suck hard, using my tongue to tease and flick.

Carlotta orgasms with a cry, arching against my mouth, and I keep stroking her with my tongue and lightly thrusting my fingers into her slick core, easing her down from the high.

Her hands drop to the floor and she moans a soft, "Oh…my…God."

I crawl up her body, drop down on my elbows, and kiss her hard, making her taste her own sweetness. "See how good you taste," I tell her, licking the seam of her lips.

"That was…intense," she murmurs.

I look into her brown eyes, so full of trust, and suddenly hate myself. I'm such an asshole and I should've kept my hands—and tongue—to myself. The temptation was just too strong, though, and I couldn't resist.

"I'm sorry," I say, feeling like the biggest piece of shit. I want her innocence, crave it on a primal level, but it's not mine to take.

She frowns. "Sorry? For what? Being the first man to go down on me?"

With a heavy sigh, I reluctantly roll off her and stare up at the ceiling. "I shouldn't have touched you."

"Oh, my God! Seriously?" She sits up, looking at me like the ferocious woman that she is. "Stop playing this hot and cold game with me. It's confusing and I don't understand how you can want me one minute… how you can do what you just did…and then push me away the next second."

"We can't get involved any deeper," I insist stubbornly. Somehow, some way, I have to figure out how to be around her and not let this powerful chemistry between us explode into something I can't handle. I've always been so focused, so strong, but Carlotta has the power to shatter all that with one kiss.

"Why?" she challenges me, eyes narrowing.

Such a feisty little thing. My thoughts instantly turn to Caitlin and how I failed her so epically. It's not something I want to talk about, so I merely shrug a shoulder and say, "I don't do relationships."

It seems like the easiest excuse to give her because I know it's not what she wants to hear. I'll protect her, but that's it. Nothing further can happen between us sexually. No matter how much my dick is arguing for the chance to sink into her sweet pussy, I have to think with the correct head.

"Don't lie to me, *Damon*. Just admit you don't want me. Not really." Before I can say another word, she gets up and runs straight out the front door, slamming it behind her.

Dammit! She doesn't have any pants or shoes on, just a pair of socks. Hell, because of me, she isn't even wearing panties. And it's way too cold out there. Gritting my teeth, I grab my coat and race out after her. But she hasn't gone far, just to the edge of the porch, and I see her shoulders shaking.

Fuck me. I made her cry. The sliver of a heart that I have left constricts painfully. "Carlotta, I'm sorry," I say in a low voice. Moving up behind her, I lay my coat over her shoulders. "Please don't cry, sweetheart. I can't bear it."

She sniffs then swipes a hand across her face as she turns around to face me. "I don't understand you. One second you seem to want me and the next you don't…because of my brothers? That's so fucking lame."

"It's more than that," I tell her. "I don't want to get into it, but I need you to understand this is about me and my issues. You're perfect, sweetheart. I'm the one who's a fucked-up asshole who isn't worthy of your virginity."

She draws the coat closer, pulling it around herself, and shivers. "I disagree. My virginity is a gift and I can give it to whomever I choose. I choose you, Damon."

Fuck me. What the hell am I supposed to say to that? She's so damn sincere and I want her more than anything. And to turn her away… well, it would just be cruel and a devastating blow to her ego.

Before I can comment, she raises a hand. "Sorry if I'm being too forward, but I feel something with you, and I thought you felt it, too. Clearly, you don't. I just have terrible luck when it comes to men. My only boyfriend—and I use the term loosely since it only lasted three months—cheated on me. He didn't want me, so I guess I'm not surprised you don't, either."

"Carlotta—"

"No, it's fine. But can I ask you a question?"

"Anything."

"Am I that undesirable? That unloveable? What's wrong with me that I'm still a virgin at twenty-five?"

"Nothing is wrong with you," I state firmly.

She snorts in disbelief.

"The truth is I desire you very much. More than I should," I admit.

"I don't believe you."

"Sweetheart, I sucked and finger fucked you into an orgasm twice in the past twenty-four hours and there's so much more I want to do. It's taking all of my self-control to not rip your clothes off right now." Stepping closer, I wrap my fingers around the edges of the coat and pull her closer, straight into my arms. "Please, don't doubt yourself because you're the most amazing woman I've ever met."

She tilts her head back, looking up at me, her eyes so full of disbelief and innocence. "Then why don't you want me?"

"I do," I grit out, tugging her closer and pressing a hard kiss against her forehead. "I'm just not the man you need."

"I do need you, Damon. I want *you* and I choose *you*. Even if that means only one night."

I pull back and search her face. Is she serious? Because if she's capable of sharing one blissful night and not expecting more then how the hell can I say no to that? Fuck, I'm standing on a slippery slope and I can feel myself sliding.

I'm going to cave in to her. It's inevitable.

"I don't want you to doubt yourself because I want you badly. More than I've ever wanted anyone," I whisper. "But I need you to understand and agree that whatever happens here stays here. Once we're back home, we go our separate ways."

"With amazing memories."

"Yeah. But I need you to be sure, Carlotta."

She pushes up onto her toes and presses her lips to mine. "I'm sure, Damon," she tells me in a low voice.

That final reassurance whispered against my mouth casts the last of my reservations into the wind. Reaching down, I scoop her up and turn, walking back into the cabin. Tonight is going to be a night that neither of us will ever forget.

I will make sure of it.

11

CARLOTTA

I made my choice and now there's no turning back. I want Damon more than anything and now I know he wants me, too. And if that means only one night then so be it. I'm ready.

He lifts me up and I wrap my legs around his waist. Once we're back inside the cabin, he kicks the door shut, locks it and carries me back over to the fireplace. Grabbing the blanket with one hand, he shakes it out, laying it down on the floor. Then he slowly lowers himself down, gently laying me back, and captures my mouth in a slow, sultry kiss that sends delicious shockwaves through my body.

I love how he can be so demanding one minute and then take it down the next, moving so slowly, so teasingly, that I want to cry. Our tongues explore and he traces the seam of my lips with his tongue then begins kissing my neck. He's taking his time, being utterly thorough, and I'm on the verge of melting into a puddle on the floor.

The moment he licks and then lightly sucks the spot right below my ear, I moan. I'm not sure why but, oh, my goodness, that spot makes me lose my mind a little.

"Is that the spot, sweetheart?" he asks, voice husky. But before I can answer, his hand slides between my legs and I lose all ability to form a coherent sentence. His fingers start stroking and I arch against his hand, needing more.

As if he can read my mind, he slips a finger, then two, inside me and thrusts them in and out. The heat and friction begin to build and when his thumb touches my clit, rubbing and finding the exact right pressure, everything in me tenses then explodes in the most beautiful way.

I cry out and he kisses me hard as he works my T-shirt up and off, tossing it aside. The fire crackles and everything is so hot—the flames, my body, his touch. The glow of the firelight illuminates my body, reminding me that I am completely naked now. He moves back, his gaze slowly sliding down my nakedness, soaking in every single curve.

"You're so fucking beautiful," he says, sliding his hands down my sides and over my hips. "I'm going to kiss every single curve on your body. Give you so much pleasure…make you scream…"

I can feel my insides turn to liquid and I need to feel his skin against mine. Reaching for his shirt, I yank it up with trembling hands and he helps, pulling it over his head. Then he lowers himself down, covering me with his heavy body, and he licks along the curve of my breast. After a minute, he makes his way over to the other one, swirling his tongue around the taut nipple. When he sucks it into his mouth, I'm glad I'm already lying down or I would've fallen to the floor when my knees buckled. It feels so damn good and I'm quivering like a bowl of jelly.

His lips, mouth and tongue are a thing of beauty and every nerve ending in my body is responding to his touches, his caresses. I'm losing myself in a sensual haze and I reach down and run my hand over the very big, very hard bulge tenting his cargo pants. When I lightly squeeze, he groans, hips thrusting forward, filling my hand with his cock which is so much bigger than I even imagined.

Oh, wow. Biting my lower lip, wrapping my legs around him, I hook a foot around his calf and try to pull him closer. Right where I need him, grinding up, circling my hips.

"Please," I murmur, not even recognizing my own voice. It's so desperate and husky, dripping with need. Just like my core.

"I'm taking my time with you," he says, moving down my body, dropping kisses everywhere.

God, I'm so overheated and all I can do is twist and turn and moan. I slide my fingers through his hair and he's nudging my legs further apart and, before I can say anything, his mouth latches onto my pussy again. Licking me into an absolute frenzy. I'm so sensitive and I'm not sure how much more of this sweet torture I can take.

"Please…I can't…" I twist and feel an intense pressure building all over again. Holy crap, this man can deliver the orgasms.

After another lick, he pulls back, moves off me and says, "Hang on, sweetheart."

My vision is hazy as I watch him walk away, his gait a little uneven, and then bend over to dig around in his duffel bag. God, that ass of his is a thing of beauty and I want to bite it. When he turns back around, I see the condom in his hand and my heart starts beating double-time. This is it—I'm lying on the floor in front of a roaring fire, naked and glistening, and I'm about to have sex. With greedy eyes, I watch him strip his cargo pants and black boxer shorts off and suck in a sharp breath.

Damon's body is even more amazing than I ever would've guessed. Literally perfect in every single way—from his chiseled face to his broad shoulders, those perfectly-carved abs and that monstrous cock standing up straight. My mouth waters.

I want him so desperately and he's about to be all mine.

For one precious night, a little voice reminds me. *So enjoy it while you can.*

Yeah, I plan to enjoy every amazing second.

Lifting my arms, reaching for him, he goes down to his knees, takes my hands and presses a kiss along my knuckles. Then he lets go, rips the package open and rolls the condom onto his length. I can't help but notice his leaking tip and the slight grimace on his face. I think he's aching just as much as I am.

He lowers onto his elbows, settling between my legs, and kisses me deeply. The first contact of his steel cock against my drenched pussy and I let out a soft, needy whimper. He left me on the edge of an orgasm and I need release just as much as he does. Arching up, trying to pull him into my body, I feel him push forward.

My body stretches and, for a moment, I panic, not sure I can accommodate him. But he immediately retreats then slides in again, this time going deeper and a sharp sting makes me gasp.

"You can take me, sweetheart. Just relax," he coaxes.

My legs drop open more and his finger finds my clit. His touch has my senses going haywire and my body responds, stretching, taking him all the way. Once he's seated fully, I dig my nails into his shoulders, trying to get used to him.

"See how good you take me?" He pulls almost all the way out and slides in again, his fingers working their unbelievable magic.

Oh, Jesus. I'm not sure how much more of this I can handle. The stinging sensation is gone and now every nerve ending is tingling, throbbing, dancing like it's competing on flipping Dancing With the Stars and doing the cha cha. Or, in this case, the horizontal mambo.

He's being slow and gentle, driving into my body with long, heavy thrusts now and it's pushing me over the edge fast. I hold on for as long as I can, but I'm no match for his experience, the skill he has over me. He's playing my body like a damn fiddle and I'm loving every second of it.

A moment later, my release hits me hard. With a cry, I ride out the wave of pleasure pouring through my body, shivers extending out every limb and ending in the tips of my fingers, toes and hair follicles. Holy God, this is better than I ever imagined it would be, but I know why. It's because of Damon. There's no doubt in my mind that his taking his time and care with me is the reason I'm shuddering with a full-body orgasm right now.

Would Rendall have done that? No way. All he ever did was give me lazy kisses and cop a feel every once in a while. He wasn't passionate like Damon. It never felt good or right and I'm so damn grateful I didn't give in and sleep with him just to unload my virginity.

Above me, Damon lifts my hips higher and starts thrusting harder, faster, chasing after his own release. It hits him fast and I look up. Our gazes lock and he stares into my eyes, into my very soul, as his hips keep pumping and he empties himself completely. His entire body stiffens then shudders. Afterward, he leans down and kisses me. It's deep and slow, and I can feel him still pulsing inside me.

I don't want this moment to ever end. I've never felt so connected to another person before. It's almost…magical.

For a long moment, neither of us moves. But then he slowly pulls out and, after another soft kiss, he gets up. I watch him walk away, unable to pull my attention off his flexing ass. He tosses the condom then grabs a dish towel. Kneeling down, he gently wipes the blood from my thighs and I swallow hard, uncomfortable because I'm not used to it, but I'm thankful.

Balling up the towel, he tosses it aside then grabs some pillows, lays back down and pulls me into his arms.

"Are you okay?" he whispers, stroking a hand over my head and down my hair. He twists his fingers around a lock, playing with it, and I sigh softly.

I nod, my cheek against his firm chest. "Yes. That was…"

"Incredible," he finishes, tightening his arms around me.

I'm glad I'm not the only one who thinks so.

Being in his arms is so comfortable, so very right, and my eyes flutter closed. He keeps playing with my hair and it's lulling me to sleep. The feel of his warm, strong arms wrapped around me, holding me close, lets me know I'm safe and, before I realize it, I'm drifting off to sleep as the fire crackles beside us.

My dreams are filled with Damon. All I can see are his dark, intense eyes and his slightly spicy smell infiltrates me. I can still taste his kisses and in my dreams I arch up into his touches. I never thought I would find someone like him. He soothes me on every level and I know we jumped into things fast, but he made it clear he can only promise me one glorious night.

Although, technically, he did say whatever happens here stays here. Kind of like Vegas. So I'm thinking if we have another couple of nights, it only makes sense to enjoy each other's company. Nothing wrong with that, right? Especially when the attraction between us is dangerously, uncontrollably combustible and burning out of control.

Whatever happens, I refuse to regret sleeping with Damon and for however long this lasts, I'm going to revel in each and every moment.

I'm not sure how long I sleep but at some point my eyes flutter open and I'm no longer in Damon's arms. It must be the middle of the night and I look over to see Damon laying next to me, staring into the fire.

"Why're you awake?" I ask, rubbing my eyes and moving closer.

"I put another log on the fire," he says. "And I didn't want to wake you up by pulling you back in for a cuddle."

I stretch out across his body. "You can always wake me—with cuddles or kisses or however you see fit."

He arches a brow. "Oh, yeah?"

"Definitely." I lazily trace a finger around his flat nipple then slide my hand through the light dusting of hair on his chest. He's so masculine and beyond sexy in every possible way. When I think about the things we did, about the things I still want to do with him, my mouth waters. "The night isn't over, you know."

He trails his fingers up and down my spine in a feather light caress. "Aren't you sore?"

"A little," I admit, "but I can think of some things that we can still do. That I can do for you."

Heat flares in his eyes. "You don't have to do anything, Carlotta. I want this night to be about you."

"But—"

"No, buts, sweetheart. If you're feeling frisky—and you're up to it—I'm going to take care of *you*."

"But what about you?"

"I'm fine for the time being."

Oh, well, that's certainly unexpected. I was inferring a blow job and I can't imagine many men would've just said what Damon did. God, he's a gentleman on top of being a consummate lover. How am I ever going to walk away from this man?

"So, tell me. Is there something you need…something you want?" he asks, voice husky. Once again, he starts toying with my hair and I let out a soft sigh.

I nod, sending him my most seductive look.

"What?"

Oh, God, he's going to make me say it. "You," I murmur, hoping to get away with that simple answer. But, of course, he doesn't accept only that.

"No, sweetheart, I need you to say the words. Tell me exactly what my dirty, little girl wants. And then I will give it to you."

There's one thing that I especially enjoyed, but how do I tell him I want oral sex? God, that's embarrassing.

"Lottie, tell me," he orders.

I let out a low breath and blink. "I want…" But the words get stuck in my throat.

"You want what, sweetheart?" He trails his hand over my ass, palming it, squeezing the flesh.

"Um, I want your mouth on me," I manage to say.

"Where exactly would you like my mouth?" When I don't respond right away, he places a kiss in my hair. "Here?"

I shake my head.

"Here?" His lips touch my bare shoulder.

I clear my throat. "Lower," I tell him and he gives me a wicked smirk.

"How about here?" His fingers trail across my stomach and circle my belly button. His index finger dips inside and I feel an electric shot zap straight through to my pussy.

"That's closer."

"Tell me, Carlotta." His hand slides lower, between my thighs and I moan.

"So close," I murmur." When he doesn't move it up to touch my dripping center, I know he's waiting for me to tell him exactly where. All I can do is surrender. "I want your mouth on my pussy, sucking me into an orgasm like you did earlier."

"What about my fingers?" he asks.

"You can use those, too."

He chuckles. "That's my good girl."

Then he drags me off his chest and lays me on my back. I watch him slide down my body which is already shaking with anticipation. His eyes meet mine and his mouth edges up. Then he slides his hands under my ass, lifting my hips off the floor, and drops his head between my legs.

And he feasts and feasts and feasts. Until I'm screaming his name and begging for mercy.

12

ARCHER

I absolutely love giving Carlotta pleasure, taking her right to the brink and then watching her explode with shudders as her release hits her. Sometimes I prolong it as long as possible, taking her to the edge then forcing her to wait in order to make it all that much more intense. But, true to my word, I keep the rest of the night all about her. As much as I'd like to sink back inside her hot, wet body, I know she's sore and I don't want to hurt her.

Hell, I figure it's the least I can do.

As strong and independent and sassy as she is, there's also a vulnerable side to the youngest Rossi. Maybe because she's always lived in the shadows of her larger than life brothers or possibly because she possesses a sweet, gentle nature that sometimes makes her shy. Whatever it is, the entire night surprises me.

She'd make a good mother, I think, lightly playing with her hair as I watch her sleep.

Oh, hell, where did that thought come from? I drop the dark brown strand and move further away. Marriage and kids are not in my future. I've always known that. My life is far too dangerous to even consider it.

Why is she making me think things that are so out of character?

Something is different about Carlotta. I like her—a lot—and didn't expect the all-consuming lust that takes over when I'm with her. And I can't deny it—the sex is outstanding. Fucking mindblowing, and I'm still trying to figure out why it is so damn good. I've slept with more experienced women who have given me nights to remember. But, out of them all, it's this little firecracker beside me that I want more from.

Fuck me. That's a very dangerous thought. *You don't want more, Archer. You got laid, you got your one night with her. Now you can both move on.*

Right?

It's easier to answer yes to that question while we're hot and heavy in front of the fireplace all night. However, when dawn breaks and light peeks in through the curtains, it's much harder. How the hell am I supposed to not touch her again? To just step away and pretend none of this ever happened?

Impossible. Especially while we're still here together.

I know one night was my brilliant idea, but I also mentioned what happens here, stays here. So, as long as we're still at the cabin, and on the same page, I figure it's okay to keep having sex. Because the honest to God's truth is being inside her only once wasn't enough.

I need more. So much more. I want to take her all over again, in different positions and various places. There's so much I want to show her, teach her.

It feels so damn good with her and I'm racking my brain to figure out why. The idea that she's never slept with anyone else except me is very appealing and brings out my possessive side even more than usual. That has to be it. It's the only explanation that makes any semblance of sense to me.

Carlotta makes a soft sound then stretches like a satisfied cat, practically purring. Her pretty dark eyes flutter open and a shy smile curves her mouth.

"Good morning," I say, loving how relaxed and content she looks. She has the expression of a very satisfied woman, thanks to me, and my chest puffs out a little. Somehow, she's always making me feel proud of myself.

"Morning." She props herself up on an elbow, holding the blanket up to her chest. I'm tempted to pull it down and suck those gorgeous breasts of hers, but I manage to restrain myself. "What're you doing up so early?"

"Admiring you."

"Oh, geez, stop. I'm a mess in the morning."

"No, you're lovely," I insist.

For a moment, we stare at each other.

"About last night…" I begin.

"Please, don't tell me you regret what we did. Please," she adds softly, "because that was probably the best night of my life."

"No, not at all, sweetheart. I just want to find out what you're thinking and how you'd like to proceed."

"Proceed?" she echoes, tilting her head.

I shrug a shoulder. "I know I said only one night, but I figure while we're here…"

My voice trails off and, from the look in her eye, she knows exactly what I'm saying. Or, in this case, not saying.

"Just so I'm clear, are you suggesting we continue last night for as long as we're at the cabin?"

I realize I'm holding my breath. If she says no, I can't blame her. But, goddamn, it's going to kill me. "Yes."

Her mouth edges up. Seductive, challenging. "Hmm. Did you have a good time last night, Archer?" she teases. So sassy.

Wicked, little thing. She knows damn well I did. "Yes. Very much so." I'm at her mercy and I wait impatiently for her decision.

She rolls onto her back. "I'm going to have to think about it," she murmurs, and I can tell by her playful tone that she isn't serious.

"Vixen," I say, then crawl over and start dropping kisses wherever I find bare skin. Her shoulder, collarbone, neck, cheek. Finally, my mouth captures hers and we kiss for several very long, delicious moments.

Carlotta pulls back, searching my face, and runs her fingers through my hair. "You're the one who keeps wanting to put a time limit on this, not me," she reminds me softly.

I look away, knowing she's right, yet also knowing it's because there's no other choice. "Because I don't want anything bad to happen to you. What I do is dangerous and the lifestyle I live isn't conducive to a relationship."

"What exactly do you do?" she asks.

"I make it my business to know things. And for the right amount of money, I'll share my intel."

She nods slowly. "And you share intel with Miceli?"

"Yes. All the time."

"He must pay you well," she surmises.

"He does."

"So you aren't actually friends with him. More like business associates."

I like Miceli, sure, but she's right. "It's safer that way," I tell her. "People who get too close to me…"

My voice trails off and she frowns.

"What?" she presses.

"They have a tendency to die," I say bluntly, and her eyes widen. "And, sweetheart, I refuse to let that happen to you. It's why we keep this—us—a secret and, yeah, we can indulge for the next few days. But that's all I can promise you."

She seems to be considering my words then nods again. "Is Archer your last name?"

"It is. It's also my call sign."

"From the military." Her fingers lightly scratch through the hair on the back of my neck. "And you said you were what branch?"

Clever thing. "I didn't say. But I was Army and then joined Delta Force."

I'm not sure why I'm answering her questions, but for whatever reason, I do. Maybe because I'm hoping it will help her to understand me better. Not that it actually matters. We're lucky if we have three whole days left together.

That thought sends a pang through my heart. It makes no sense and I don't understand it, but I'd be lying if I denied it.

"I don't know much about Delta Force. What does it do?"

"It's an elite special operations unit. My team did the highly secretive stuff. We took out high value targets, dismantled terrorist cells, rescued hostages. A lot of cover missions where we worked directly with the CIA. Direct action missions, too."

"What are those?"

"Raids, sabotage, that kind of thing," I tell her. No one has ever asked me about my time in Delta and I never planned on telling anyone. But something about Carlotta makes me want to talk, to open up that part of myself which I locked down years ago after leaving spec ops.

"Did you like it?"

I think carefully over her question before answering. "Yes and no. The training was top notch and taught me everything I needed to know about taking down the enemy. My team was the best. I made a lot of great connections and maintained them. It's one of the reasons I can find out information so quickly and easily. And nothing gave me greater satisfaction than eliminating another bad guy."

"I'm hearing a 'but' in there," she says quietly.

"But it took its toll. Some days, it's still taking its toll."

"How? Do you mean like with nightmares? Or regrets?"

"Neither," I tell her, trying to figure out the best way to explain what I mean. "I don't regret anything I've done or had to do to protect others. And I don't lose sleep over the evil men I've killed."

"Then what do you mean it took its toll?"

"Because of what I've done and been through, it's impossible for me to have a normal relationship." She frowns and I can tell she doesn't believe me. "I'm broken, Carlotta. In such a significant way that I can't ever feel whole again. I accept who I am and what I've done, but I don't expect anyone else to settle for whatever pieces are left of me."

"I think sometimes two broken people can come together and help each other. They can fill the holes and empty spaces. They can offer their pieces and, somehow, they complete each other."

"Maybe in the movies and books. But in real life, that just doesn't happen. There is no happily ever after for someone like me."

"Maybe you need to have a little faith, Damon Archer."

I'm done talking about such serious stuff and wasting time. I'll never be able to be fixed and it doesn't matter what Carlotta believes. I know the sad truth and nothing can truly repair my soul. I've seen and done too much.

"I'm a faithless man, Lottie." I keep my tone light and slap her ass. "Now how about some coffee? Maybe a walk in the woods this morning?"

I get up and walk toward the small kitchen, swiping up my pajama bottoms on the way. I can feel her eyes on my backside and I glance over my shoulder.

"See something you like, sweetheart?" I ask.

"Yes," she purrs, also standing up. But she keeps the blanket wrapped around her naked body. I catch glimpses of skin here or there, but definitely not enough.

"Why don't you leave that blanket out here?" I suggest, slipping on my bottoms as she heads to the bathroom.

She lets out a low, throaty chuckle. "Oh, you'd like that, wouldn't you?"

"You bet your sweet, biteable ass, I would," I growl.

"Biteable?" She arches a brow. "You wouldn't dare."

"You don't think so?" I challenge.

The moment I round the island and start toward her, she squeals, races into the bathroom and shuts the door.

"You better run," I murmur under my breath, my dick getting hard when I think of all the things we have yet to do.

I hope she's ready because I don't plan to waste one single minute over the next few days. I plan to take full advantage of that luscious body of hers and make sure she's satisfied in every possible way.

13

CARLOTTA

Staring at myself in the mirror as I brush my teeth, I come to several conclusions. First, I look happier than I've ever been before. Truly like a woman who was fucked good and well, and that's a first for me which makes it slightly delicious. My cheeks glow and there's a pleasant buzz moving just beneath my skin. Like a current that has my entire body tingling. I can still feel a twinge between my legs, but it's not unpleasant. It's just a sexy reminder of how big Damon is and what he can do with that magical cock of his. I'm glad I waited for him and his experience made last night unforgettable in every way.

Second, it makes me happy that he's beginning to open up to me. If I had to guess, I'd say he probably rarely, if ever, confides in anyone. Maybe by talking about his past, he can find some kind of healing. He said he's broken and I'll do whatever I can to help him feel whole again. No matter what he thinks about himself, I know he's a good man. A protector to his core who will defend the people he loves.

And, third, I'm going to enjoy every moment we have up here, isolated in this cabin together. He's adamant we can't see each other again once we return to the city, but I'm not onboard with that idea at all. In fact, my plan is to slowly make him see how good we are together. Because if last night is any indication, I don't see how he could just walk away.

I can smell the yummy scent of brewing coffee and I'm ready for the caffeine jolt. After changing back into Damon's sweatpants and T-shirt and pulling my hair up into a messy bun, I walk out of the bathroom and head over to the island where he sits.

Pulling out the stool beside him, I drop down and reach for the steaming mug waiting for me. I lift it up, blow lightly, and take a sip. "Thank you," I say. I'm used to sweet, flavored coffee, but surprisingly, I realize that I don't mind this plain black stuff.

"You're welcome."

I glance over at him from the corner of my eye and my heart kicks up a notch. He's starting to affect me and that's scary. Especially since he doesn't want anything long term. But how can I not be affected by him? His dark stubble is thicker now, a light beard, and I can still remember how it felt scraping against my inner thighs. His long fingers are wrapped around his mug and he lifts it up, touches his mouth to the side and drinks. That same mouth that latched onto my pussy last night again and again and made me scream.

I'm getting hot and bothered, and I really need to cool off.

"How about that walk?" I suggest.

He looks over and smirks as though he can hear my salacious thoughts.

"You ready?"

I nod. "Yep. Can I take my coffee with me?"

He gives me a funny look. "Of course. You can do whatever you want."

I guess it was a silly question, but I'm so used to asking for permission before I do something. I don't really know why. Maybe because I'm the youngest and I'm used to being bossed around. Or maybe because it's the polite thing to do.

"Make sure to bundle up," he tells me and finishes the rest of his coffee. "It's going to be chilly out there."

I follow him over to the closet and he pulls out a jacket and a scarf for me. I wrap myself up and watch as he slips his leather jacket on.

"What about you?" I ask and nudge him with my shoulder.

"I don't need any extra layers. You're making me hot enough."

A pleasant blush warms my cheeks as we walk outside. I'm glad to know he's as affected as I am. We head down the steps and I look up at the perfect sky above. It's sunny, not a cloud in all that azure beauty, but it's definitely cold. One of those brisk, late fall days where the leaves crunch beneath your feet and thoughts of hot cocoa fill your head. The holidays are approaching fast and I wonder who Damon plans to spend them with since he doesn't have any family. The idea of him being alone bothers me. A lot.

So much, in fact, that I decide to bring it up.

Damon leads us away from the cabin and toward the woods. "This way," he says, pointing out a path.

"I can't believe how fast this year has flown by. It's going to be Christmas before you know it."

He merely nods.

"Any holiday plans this year?" I ask, looking over at his chiseled profile. I suck in a breath, admiring him. He's really far too handsome for his own good.

"Not really," he responds. "Christmas is just like any other day, you know?"

My chest tightens. It's not, though. It should be spent with friends and family, exchanging gifts, eating together, making memories.

Damon Archer doesn't have that and my heart breaks a little for him.

He glances over at me. "I bet the Rossi's all gather together and celebrate, huh?"

"Yes. We all go to Sicily to be with Mom and Dad. It's magical over there during the holidays—all decorated and there are so many traditions everyone follows."

"Like what?" he asks, looking interested.

"Well, outside of the churches, they hold live nativities and they light bonfires to keep baby Jesus warm. And there are processions. A big one is for Santa Lucia in Syracuse and the streets are filled with candles and poinsettias. December in Sicily is amazing."

"It sounds nice," he says, voice turning quieter, thoughtful.

"It is. But as long as I'm with my family, I don't care where we are." I briefly hesitate then blurt out, "You know, you're always welcome to join us."

For a long moment, he doesn't say anything and I begin to feel foolish for offering. But then he reaches for my hand, threading his fingers through mine and says, "Thank you. That's a very sweet offer."

I squeeze my eyes closed and try to ignore the way I'm responding to him…to his touch…to his words. I like him way more than I should and I feel myself moving into very dangerous territory.

This is supposed to be a fling, I sternly remind myself.

Well, if that's all it is, then what the hell are we doing on a hike? We should be in bed. I'm ready for round two and I need to let him know, just in case he's holding back because he thinks he might hurt me.

I abruptly stop walking, yank him closer and look up into his surprised eyes. Not wanting to waste one more second, I grab his leather coat and push up onto my toes. "Put your mouth on mine, Damon," I order huskily.

Heat flares between us and I don't have to ask twice. His mouth crashes against mine and it's a scorching kiss full of need. He lifts me up off the ground and I wrap my legs around his waist. We devour each other and I roll my hips against his, letting him know I want him. Now.

Passion consumes us. Pushing my back against a nearby tree, he slips a hand straight down my panties and I shamelessly rub against him.

"Oh, shit, sweetheart. You're so wet."

My fingers curl into his jacket, my nails no doubt leaving half moon-shaped marks in the leather. He's stroking me, creating an absolute frenzy, and I whimper when he slides his fingers inside my soaked core. I'm slick and aching, wanting the release that only he can provide.

"God, Damon…please…" I moan, his fingers thrusting and working my clit at the same time.

"What do you need, sweetheart?"

He's going to make me say it, to tell him, and this time I have zero shame or hesitation. Reaching down, I wrap my hand around his hard cock and squeeze. "I want your cock deep in my pussy. Now," I demand.

My quick, naughty reply must surprise him because his fingers stop moving and he smiles against my lips.

"That's my girl. Never hold back telling me what you want."

"And what do you want?" I fire back, palming him more firmly.

"Fuck, babe, I want it all," he rasps, ripping my sweats and panties off.

I'm tugging at his pants, fumbling to get them down as quickly as possible because I'm salivating for this man. Hot and desperate and so full of wanton desire. "I want that, too."

He helps me shove them down and his glorious cock springs free. Lifting me higher, his engorged tip touches my entrance and I grasp his shoulders tightly and sink down as he thrusts up.

We both let out a low groan and I tighten my legs around his waist, my back propped against the rough bark. But the coat protects it and I lift up then plunge back down, taking him to the hilt.

"I need you," I whisper against his lips. "Hard and fast. Please..."

"Then that's what you'll get," he assures me. "Hold on, sweetheart."

He grabs my hips, fingers digging into my sides, and then starts thrusting up. This time, he doesn't hold back and I gasp. Maybe it's a little too much but, oh, my God, it feels amazing. Slightly wild and unrestrained, his powerful hips pump, stretching me to the max, making me take every single inch.

It's rough and all brutal strength, and I love it. Even better than the night before.

"Yes, oh, God, yes," I cry, pulling him home with every single hard thrust. I feel like I'm going to burst into a ray of light.

I have no idea how he can manage to hold me up, angle our bodies just right and keep pounding into me, but I don't care. He is clearly multi-talented because he also manages to find my sweet spot, hitting it again and again. I cry out, tightening my arms around him, clinging to his big, strong body for dear life. My pussy clenches hard, milking him, and I drop my head back as my release slams into me with the force of a hurricane.

Yep, Hurricane Archer just landed and I scream his name to the nearly-bare branches of the trees above us.

I can feel the moment his control snaps and it's delicious. He curses, groans against my neck and bites the soft skin there, immediately soothing it with his tongue as his entire body shudders and erupts.

But then I notice a different sensation. It belatedly occurs to me that he just exploded inside me…without protection. My eyes squeeze closed and we rock against each other as he fills me, coming hard. Wet, hot, pulsing spurts.

The idea of getting pregnant suddenly becomes very real. And if we only promised each other a few days then what the hell are we doing?

That's what my logical side says. But my pussy is weeping and squeezing him tightly, and she's fucking deliriously happy. I suppose she's always been an illogical hussy.

Well, what's done is done. He lifts his head and our gazes lock, both of us knowing the possible ramifications of what we just did. But he doesn't pull out, just stays seated deep inside me, and then he captures my mouth in a slow, deep kiss that makes my toes curl.

Without a doubt, I know I'm falling for him. And I'm falling so damn hard and fast, it's scary. For a long moment, we hold each other and keep kissing as though our very lives depended on it. After what feels like forever, he slowly lifts me up, pulling out and sets me back on my feet.

"We didn't use anything," I whisper.

"I know better. I'm sorry. If anything happens—"

"We'll figure it out," I interrupt, reaching down to grab my panties and slipping them back on. It's hot, sticky and wet between my legs, but I try to ignore it. It's sort of hard to ignore his semen dripping out of my body, though, but I do my best to act casual.

After we're fully dressed again, he pulls me close and kisses me hard.

"I shouldn't have taken you bare and I never do that. I want you to know I'm clean and haven't had unprotected sex since Caitlin."

"Caitlin?" I frown.

"My old girlfriend. We dated five years ago."

"Oh." I mean, what the hell am I supposed to say to that? We just had ridiculously amazing sex without a condom and now he's telling me his old girlfriend's name when I could possibly be pregnant.

My face falls.

"Carlotta?"

"Hmm?"

"Look at me, sweetheart."

When I don't move, he places a couple of fingers under my chin, lifting it up, forcing me to make eye contact.

"If anything happens, I won't abandon you."

I nod, grateful, but at the same time, stewing in jealousy over a girl he slept with five years ago. It's silly and doesn't make any logical sense. Especially since we've promised each other nothing. Well, nothing but a few glorious days of fucking.

Yet, I can feel myself wanting more—needing more—from him. And that's leading me into very dangerous territory.

"There are plenty of options nowadays," I say absently, even though I know I'd never go through with an abortion. Ending the life of an innocent baby? No way. The guilt would haunt me forever. Plus, the idea of a child that is half me and half him…

I chew on my lower lip, liking the idea far more than I should.

Damon doesn't comment and we start walking again. With each step, I'm reminded of what we just did. I'm sore and my panties are soaked. Walking away from this without getting knocked up would be a miracle because that man just fucked me so hard my legs are jelly and my vision is still hazy.

In my head, I quickly calculate where I am in my cycle and if pregnancy is even a real possibility.

Fuck. The answer is yes. A very resounding yes. Honestly, I don't think we could have scheduled a better time to do it because I should be ovulating right now. Biting down on my fingernail, I realize five minutes of getting pounded against a tree might've just changed the entire course of my life.

And yet I don't regret one single moment. In fact, if having his baby means keeping Damon in my life then I'm fine with that. Because I've come to realize he's a wounded man and there's nothing I want more than to help him.

I know better than anyone that sometimes family can help in the most miraculous way. They give you a home and a place where you can always safely retreat and regroup after the world becomes too harsh. They don't judge you and they love you fiercely.

Maybe that's exactly what Damon needs. A good family who will embrace him.

14

ARCHER

After our walk in the woods, or maybe I should say our romp in the woods, Carlotta and I return to the cabin. She tells me she's going to go take a shower and all sorts of dirty thoughts and images fill my head. I can't stop thinking about the larger rustic shower, its water raining down on her naked body. I know our time is running out and I want to make the most of it.

Being the insatiable beast that I am, I shed my clothes, make sure to grab a condom this time, and stroll into the bathroom. She glances over, eyes widening then smiles in welcome.

"Mind if I join you?" I ask huskily and make my way over.

"I was hoping you would," she says, her eyes skating down my body. I'm already half hard and there's definitely no hiding it.

I pull Carlotta into my arms and for the next forty minutes, I find myself lost in her, lost in a heaven I've never known before. It's why I can't seem to get enough of her. There's something so incredible that happens when we're together, the moment our bodies join, and it's beyond indescribable. Unlike anything I've ever experienced before.

All I know is she fills the empty spaces and I don't feel so damaged or so alone anymore.

Once the water runs cool, I turn it off, grab a towel and wrap her up. Then I carry her to the loft's bedroom and lay her out on the bed. Stretching out beside her, we kiss and touch and explore each other's bodies thoroughly. As though we have all the time in the world.

After spending most of the day in bed, I'm ravenously hungry. We decide to go down to the kitchen and whip up some easy comfort food. Our options are limited, but I find a big frozen pizza and nothing ever tasted so good. We devour it and talk while we eat. I've never opened up this much to a woman before, but I trust Carlotta. I even tell her about my uncle who I lived with after my parents died.

"Uncle Bill was former Army and I'm grateful he took me in when I had nowhere else to go, but he wasn't an affectionate man. He fed me, put a roof over my head and made sure I went to school, and that's about it."

"All children need to know they're loved," Carlotta says, "with words and gestures. My family is so affectionate. Always hugging and teasing. I can't imagine it being anything different."

"My uncle didn't have any siblings and my aunt couldn't have children, so I don't think he knew what to do with me, to be honest. I came to him after Aunt Sue had already died and half the time I think he wished he could've handed me over to an orphanage or something."

"That's awful."

"He wasn't a bad person. He just…ignored me."

And sometimes that's the worst thing someone can do to a kid. Hell, to anyone. Making someone feel invisible and like they don't matter is a terrible feeling.

"I'm so sorry, Damon." She lays a hand over mine.

"Not much I could do about it," I say with a shrug. "It's probably why I'm such a loner. I don't need much when it comes to people and relationships."

She lightly squeezes my hand. "You need more than you think and you're worthy of love and affection."

My chest tightens—or maybe it's my normally cold, empty heart—and her words hit me hard, on a visceral level. Is she right? Am I worthy? For so long I've kept myself closed off to others, alway telling myself I don't need anyone, that life is simpler when I'm alone. Thoughts of Caitlin hit me like a sucker punch and I drop my slice of pizza, my appetite shot to hell.

I can still picture her body laying on the floor in the bedroom, her blood soaking through the beige carpet. Crimson stains that would never come out and a horrific image that would be forever burned in my head.

"What's wrong?" she asks softly, picking up on my heavy feelings.

The urge to tell her makes me talk. I've never confided in anyone about Caitlin's death, and I haven't talked about it since the police arrived that long ago day five years earlier.

"I had a girlfriend once," I tell Carlotta in a low voice, and she leans forward, listening closely. "Her name was Caitlin."

I let out a sigh, always wishing the situation could've ended differently. That I would've had the balls to break up with her when I knew things weren't working out. But I guess I always knew deep down that we didn't have a future together. Our relationship was a here and now type of thing, nothing I ever viewed as permanent and leading to marriage and kids. But instead of facing her like a man and ending things, I always just ran away on the next op.

"Yes, you mentioned her. What happened?" she asks softly.

Our fingers thread together and I look down, needing her touch more than she realizes. "Well, I learned I was a terrible boyfriend."

"Why do you say that?"

"I always put my job first which I had to do while a spec ops guy. We had to pick up leave at a moment's notice. That's just the way it was, what I signed up for. But, with hindsight, I realize that I used my job as an excuse, a crutch."

She waits patiently while I gather my thoughts, trying to figure out the best way to share my story. The best way to let her know what an asshole I was.

"We moved in together and after a few months, I could feel myself drifting away. Maybe I lost interest or maybe it was because I was so focused on work. But I knew I should break up with her. I didn't, though, because I didn't want to deal with her getting upset and the drama of her moving out and probably hating me. So instead of facing our failed relationship, I ran off on missions and took my anger and frustration out on the enemy."

God, I wish I had a beer. Having to face my past failures sober is a little daunting. And sharing them with Carlotta? Not the easiest thing I've ever done. In fact, it's fucking brutal and makes me feel like the lowest kind of heel.

"So, I was gone on an op and the entire time, I kept thinking about how I was going to break it off with her when I got back. I was determined to do it this time. Sometimes things don't work out, that's life, right? I just didn't want to pretend anymore. Maybe we both knew it was over. I don't know. Normally, on my way home, I'd usually call to give her a heads-up, but I didn't bother this time. My phone rang when I was almost home and I saw her name, but…I didn't answer. I figured I'd see her in a couple of minutes, right? When I pulled in the driveway, I parked and sat there for a minute, getting ready to face her to tell her it was over."

My gut churns at the memory.

"How'd she take it?"

"She never got to hear my spiel. Halfway up the driveway, I noticed the front door was ajar. I dropped my duffel bag, grabbed my Glock and went inside. The place was a mess, like somebody had trashed it. Things were missing, broken, and I knew we'd been robbed. I remember calling her name, moving through the house, but she didn't answer."

I pause and pull in a deep steadying breath. Carlotta is still holding my hand and it gives me the strength to continue.

"I could feel something was wrong and when I stepped into the bedroom, I saw her. Laying on the floor in a pool of blood, a couple of gunshot wounds to the chest. Her cell phone was clutched in her hand. She'd tried calling me and I ignored it."

"Oh, God."

"I was too late. She was already gone, the robbers were already gone and there was nothing I could do except call the police. Eventually, they caught the assholes responsible and they went to prison for her murder. I left the military not long after because my focus was all over the place. I blamed myself for what happened. I wasn't there and I know I could've prevented it. I would've stopped those assholes and Caitlin would still be alive."

"It's not your fault," Carlotta says softly. "And what if you couldn't have stopped them? You might've been hurt or worse."

"I would've fucking stopped them with a bullet to the head. I promise you that," I state darkly, and I can't miss the shiver that runs through her body.

"Maybe, but you have no idea what might've happened. It was a horrible thing that occurred, but you can't blame yourself."

"I do, though. Every single day for the past five years. And I hate myself for not being there to protect her and even more for wanting to break up with her."

"Oh, Damon, I'm so sorry you had to go through that. But, please believe me when I say it wasn't your fault. It was a tragedy, pure and simple, and it had nothing to do with you wanting to end things."

"I never loved her," I admit in a low, tortured voice. "She would say the words so freely and I couldn't even choke them out. She told me I'd say them when I was ready, but I wasn't able to give her what she wanted or deserved. I never said them. I don't think I'm capable of such a deep emotion. Not with anybody."

Our eyes meet and she shakes her head.

"You loved your parents, right?" she asks.

"I guess. It was so long ago and I barely remember them. I've just accepted my brokenness, Carlotta. Nothing can fix me."

Carlotta lets go of my hand and stands up, hands going on her hips. So feisty, so determined to prove me wrong. "Love can fix you, Damon Archer. It can seal the cracks and mend your soul. Don't doubt its power. I've seen its healing strength firsthand with all of my brothers." Her voice lowers, becoming more gentle. "Maybe it's not always romantic love. It could be a friend's love or a family's love or a child's love. Promise me you won't give up on yourself."

I reach my hands out and she instantly takes them. "How did you get so wise?" I ask, tugging her onto my lap.

"I am wise," she declares saucily, cupping my face, looking right into my eyes. "And my first pearl of wisdom to you is to kiss the woman in your arms immediately."

"That seems like pretty sound advice," I tease.

"Oh, it is," she assures me with a mischievous grin.

Unable to resist, I capture her mouth in a kiss that soothes my soul and gives my heart hope. Maybe she's right. Perhaps one day I will be able to forgive myself and let go of the past. Right now, though, I'm determined to just enjoy the present. I don't want to think about the future, either. All I want to do is absorb Carlotta's light and positive energy.

At some point, I know this perfect bubble we've created is going to pop. I just don't expect it to be quite so soon. The kiss leads to a steamy encounter on the kitchen island and we're still riding high on our releases when my phone rings. I yank up my sweats and grab it up off the kitchen table.

"Archer," I answer, my gaze sliding down Carlotta's slim legs. She's just wearing my T-shirt and taking her on the countertop was the best dessert I could've asked for.

"It's Miceli."

"Hey, Miceli, let me put you on speaker." I turn the speaker on and we both sit down at the table. "What's up? Any word on Gallo?"

"That's why I'm calling. The bastard has done a disappearing act. No one can locate him and that makes us nervous."

I exchange a look with Carlotta. "So you want us to hang out up here a little longer?" I have zero problems with that and reach for her hand. We smile at each other and I'm already starting to think about how many wicked things we can do to each other for the next week. Hell, maybe even longer. I'm going to take her on every surface in this cabin.

"No," he says, interrupting my dirty thoughts. "We want to keep Carlotta safe, so we decided the best option is to send her to Sicily to stay with our parents until Gallo can be handled."

"What?" Carlotta practically screeches.

"Hi, Lottie," Miceli says dryly.

"Don't you 'hi' me," she says, getting angry fast. "We're perfectly safe up here and I don't want to run all the way to Sicily and hide."

"Sorry, sis. The jet is waiting and Archer is going to take you back to the city to pack a bag then go straight to the airport. No arguments. Your safety is our top priority, especially after Gallo managed to kidnap you earlier. Or, have you conveniently forgotten that?"

"Of course I haven't forgotten," she snaps. Then she immediately gentles her voice. "But, Miceli, I feel safe here."

"I'm glad, but you're going to Sicily."

She's steaming mad, of course, but I can't go against Miceli. Carlotta is his sister and getting her out of the country is probably the best move. But this is the moment I've been dreading. Saying goodbye to Carlotta is going to suck in the worst way possible. Over the past few days, I've grown to like her so much. The more I get to know about her, the more time I want to spend with her. But that's all coming to an end.

I glance down at my watch. "We'll leave immediately," I tell Miceli, and Carlotta slams a fist against the table, but I ignore her.

"Thanks, Archer. And, Carlotta?"

"What?" she grates out between clenched teeth.

"Behave yourself and we'll see you in December for the holidays."

Before she can make an angry retort, we both disconnect the call.

"Carlotta, he's right. Whether you like it or not, going to Sicily is the safest course of action."

"So you're just fine with this?"

No, but what can I say?

"I have to be," I tell her. "Your brothers put your care in my hands and I won't jeopardize that for a few more fucks."

The moment the words leave my mouth, I regret them. Instantly.

Shit.

Her dark eyes narrow, brows drawing down and jaw clenching. "Oh, right. We're just fucking here so no big deal, right? Plus, hey, what a great way to get rid of me—do my brother's bidding."

"That's not what I meant," I say, trying to back track. "I don't want to get rid of you. I'm enjoying our time together here and…" My voice trails off at the furious look on her face.

I keep digging myself deeper and I probably should shut up.

"I'm sure you are," she says scathingly then stands up. "Good to know you had fun fucking me, but let's go. My brothers have spoken."

As she stalks away, I know better than to comment. At least if I don't want her to rip me a new one. My little hurricane just landed and I need to batten down the hatches. It's going to be a stormy ride back to NYC, that's for sure.

15

CARLOTTA

I start to march to the front door, but Damon grabs my arm, spinning me around to face him.

"Your brothers put your care in my hands and I won't jeopardize that for a few more fucks."

Maybe he's right but, wow, that really stung. For as much as we've gotten to know each other this past week, that sentence makes me wonder if we're even remotely on the same page. Or planet. Despite our agreeing that what happens up north stays up north, my foolish heart was hoping for a different outcome.

"Carlotta, wait," he says. "I need you to understand your safety is of the utmost concern to myself and your family. Gallo is still out there and you need to be taken somewhere safe."

"I understand that, but I'm not the only one he wants. He said he's going to destroy the entire Rossi family—that includes me, my brothers, their wives and children, right? Yet why am I the only one getting put on a plane and sent over to Sicily?"

"Your brothers can protect their wives and kids. You don't have that."

His reminder is like nails down a chalkboard. He's basically telling me he won't be with me once we return to the city, and even though I know that, suddenly I'm livid. At him, at my brothers, at Gallo and the situation.

"Let's go then," I hiss, spinning back around. I'm spitting angry and I know it isn't fair. Everyone is just trying to protect me, but I can't help it. This whole thing just further emphasizes that I'm alone, vulnerable and it's time to run back to my parents because I don't have a husband or boyfriend to protect me. Because clearly this family thinks the women all need to be guarded by a man or else they're helpless. Easing pickings. *Grr.*

Gritting back my frustration, I mentally duel with the double-edged sword of my femininity while Damon gathers his stuff and shoves it into his duffel bag, preparing for our departure. Since I don't have anything, except for my dress, I just sit there and stew in my anger.

Being a woman in the Rossi family isn't an easy thing, especially when I have four overprotective brothers breathing down my neck all the time. I appreciate their concern but, at the same time, they need to understand I can be trusted to make my own decisions. Because I think that's what is upsetting me the most—I am getting zero say in what is happening.

And that's frustrating beyond anything else.

Once Damon is ready, we step outside and he locks up. I can't pretend I'm not going to miss this little cabin and the time we spent here. It was truly magical. But cold, hard reality just clunked me upside the head and now it's time to say goodbye to everything that has made me so happy this past week.

And, unfortunately for me, I'm not ready to do that.

I get in the Challenger while he tosses the duffel bag into the trunk and I sigh heavily. A part of me is furious that my brothers are forcing me to go hide in Sicily with my parents, a bigger part is grateful because I know they mean well, and an even bigger part of me is angry at Damon for following their demands and ignoring what I want and need.

Maybe I'm being a brat or maybe I'm being a woman trying to assert her independence. Whatever the case, I feel like arguing and letting my frustrations out, and the only person I can fight with is Damon.

As soon as he settles into the driver's seat and starts the car, I turn to face him. I hope he's ready because I have a lot to say. And he's probably not going to like any of it.

"You do realize you're acting like Miceli's lapdog," I tell him.

A muscle flexes in his jaw, but he refrains from commenting.

"Even though they like to think they know everything, my brothers aren't the boss of me."

"You're going to Sicily," he states in a firm voice. "Nothing you can say is going to change that."

"What if I refuse?"

"Carlotta, Gallo's thugs already got you once. Your family doesn't want that to happen again which means it's my job to get that ass of yours on the jet waiting to take you to a safe place. Now stop being a brat or so help me…"

His voice trails off on that threat and I sit up straighter. "Or what? What do you think you'd do?"

"I don't think anything," he says darkly, turning to glance over at me. "I'm saying that if you continue to act like a brat then I'm going to treat you like one."

"And what exactly does that mean?" I press. I'm striving for whiny, but my voice starts sounding husky.

"It means I'm going to spank your ass and drag you onto that plane."

I suck in a breath and I know his words aren't supposed to turn me on, but they do. His palm on my rear end is hardly a threat. I'd like it there.

"I'm not scared of you, Damon. And your threat…well, I think it's having the opposite effect that you intend."

He merely grunts and turns his attention back to the road.

But I'm not letting him off the hook that easily. "Because what if I want you to spank me? What if the idea of your hand on my ass is making me wet and—"

"Jesus, Carlotta. Enough." His voice sounds strained and I don't miss the way he shifts in his seat. He's just as uncomfortable as I am. Aching like I'm aching.

"Is it, though, Damon? Enough?" I press. "Because no matter how many times you came inside me, I'm still craving more. Still wanting to feel the pleasure only you can give me."

"We agreed once we went back to the city, you and I would go our separate ways," he reminds me, but he doesn't sound quite as convinced as he was before. Probably because it's a terrible idea.

"I know what you said, but it's not what I want. I think we owe it to each other to explore whatever this is more fully. Don't you?"

But he shakes his head. So damn stubborn. "No," he grits out. "It's impossible. You're leaving and I already told you I can't do that."

"Why? Because of what happened with Caitlin? This is totally different—"

"I don't want a relationship with you, Carlotta." My heart crumbles within my chest at his cruel words and then his voice softens. But, it's already too late. "I can't. I'm sorry. I thought I made that clear."

For a long moment I don't say anything. Then the most random thought occurs to me. "I left my dress at the cabin."

"I can send it to you," he offers.

"Don't bother," I reply sadly. "I don't want to be reminded of that night. Or of you."

From the corner of my eye, I think I see him visibly flinch. But maybe it's just my imagination. After all, I did imagine he would want to try seeing each other once we got back home. Clearly, I was sorely mistaken and that hurts more than I can express.

Perhaps this entire week was nothing more than a distraction for him. It meant so much more to me, but that's because I allowed myself to be vulnerable. Big mistake. Turning away from him, I draw my legs up and stare out the window for the rest of the ride home. There's nothing more to say and my heart is breaking on every level for what could've been.

When we reach the city, I give him directions to my apartment in the Village and he almost looks surprised. "What?" I ask as he pulls up to the curb.

"Nothing," he says. "I just didn't realize how close you are to my place."

How convenient would that be if we were dating? I want to ask him where exactly he lives, but what's the point? Getting out of the car, I shut the door and he follows me up to the building. I sigh, unlock the main door and then continue on to my apartment.

"Don't expect anything fancy," I warn him, unlocking my door. "I'm not nearly as extravagant as the rest of my family."

"I don't live on Billionaire's Row, either," he murmurs as we step inside and he looks around.

"It's all I need. And it's cozy."

He nods, walking into the living room, checking it out.

"I'll go pack."

"Do it quickly, okay?"

"Wow. You can't wait to get rid of me," I state, my tone flat.

"It has nothing to do with getting rid of you," he says. "This place isn't safe and the sooner we leave, the better."

"Yeah, yeah," I grumble and head down to my bedroom. All of my life, I've been bossed around and, dare I say, taken for granted. A part of me wants to stand my ground and put up a fight. A fight to stay here at my home and a fight to keep Damon.

Maybe I should start referring to him as Archer again. It might help me put space between us. It also hurts to consider.

Walking into my room, I look around, focus on my bed, and sigh heavily. *That bed could've seen so much action,* I think sadly. *Oh, well.* I'm used to sleeping alone, so it'll be back to business as usual. Or, maybe I should say back to no business as usual.

I open my closet and pull my suitcase out, debating what I should bring with me on the trip when I hear a sound behind me. Glancing over my shoulder, I see Damon standing in the doorway.

"Hurry up, Carlotta," he tells me, and I frown.

"Why? What's the big hur—"

The rest of the sentence gets stuck in my throat when I hear a loud crash from the other room. It sounds like someone just broke the door down with a battering ram. I jump a mile and my stomach sinks sickeningly like I'm tipping over the first gigantic hill of a roller-coaster as Damon pulls his gun.

"Shut the door!" he hisses, rushing back toward the living room.

I wish I could say I listen well, but I don't. Instead, I hurry after him, but it's only because I'm scared for him and I want to help. I refuse to be a helpless female who runs and hides in the closet, hoping the bad guys don't find her.

No way. That's not me. As I run after Damon, I grab the racquet from my closet that I use when Angelo and I play racquetball every week, and I get ready to bash some assholes. Because I am not going down without a fight. If I've learned anything from my brothers, it's to never show fear or back down in the face of a threat whether it's in business or my personal life.

I'm not stupid, either. I know I'm probably smaller than most men and I'm not carrying a gun. Tightening my grip on the racquet's handle, I skid to a halt in the archway leading out to the living room and momentarily freeze.

Three men are fighting Damon and in no world is that a fair fight. He's doing a great job, swinging punches and launching kicks, but where the hell is his gun? I step forward, my gaze scanning the floor and then I see it. It lays near the couch, part of it hidden beneath, and must've gotten knocked out of his hands.

While Damon fights the thugs off, I sprint over to the couch. Just as I bend down to grab the gun, someone moves up behind me and shoves something into my back.

"Don't move," a deep voice growls.

Terror fills me because I know it must be the barrel of a gun. I automatically lift my hands in the air as Damon gives a pained shout.

Oh, God.

Glancing over my shoulder, I see him fall to the floor. His body twitches and I realize one of the thugs has taken him down with a stun gun. Panic threatens to consume me and all I can think about is his safety. If they shoot him while he's immobilized, I will never forgive myself. Never get over it.

"Stop!" I yell. "Leave him alone!"

All eyes turn to me and I swallow hard.

"It's me you want, not him. Don't touch him and I'll go with you. But if you lay one hand on him, I will fight and scream and you'll have to shoot me dead first."

I wave the racquet in front of me for good emphasis because I am not messing around. My gut knows Damon's life is on the line and I need to protect him.

"Why're you just standing there gawking? Let's go, you idiots. Take me to Carmine Gallo like the good little thugs you are," I taunt.

A strong hand wraps around my upper arm, squeezing it tightly. "You heard the bitch," he growls. "The sooner we take her to Gallo, the sooner we get paid."

"What about him?" the big guy asks, nudging a boot against Damon. Blood drips from the thug's nose and I'm glad Damon managed to get a good hit in before the stun gun took him down.

"Leave him. He's not our problem," the other man responds then rips the racquet from my hands and throws it across the room. "But juice him again."

As Gallo's man drags me out of the apartment, I see the big guy stun Damon again then kick him hard in his side and my heart cries out. But at least I convinced them to leave him alone. *He's going to be okay,* I tell myself. He has to be.

Me, though? Well, I have my doubts. Gallo is hellbent on revenge and it looks like he's determined to take me out first.

But you better believe I will give him a piece of my mind before he does it. And I will not go out without a fight.

16

ARCHER

Lying on the floor, I am aware of everything happening around me, but I can't move. The stun gun temporarily scrambled my neural signals. Immobilized and helpless, I hear Carlotta yell at them to leave me alone, but I prepare myself to get a bullet in the head. Miraculously, it doesn't happen. After another jolt, they leave me breathing and take Carlotta.

Big mistake. Big fucking mistake.

My mind reels as my muscles contract, trying to work, but failing miserably. I should've known it was a mistake to come here. I started getting antsy after Carlotta went into her bedroom. Those thugs must've been keeping an eye on her apartment.

But I'm still breathing which means I'm going to save my woman. Because, yeah, at some point Carlotta Rossi became mine. Maybe she belonged to me the moment we kissed at the masquerade party. I don't know. All I do know is I'm going to have to do some serious groveling and hope she'll forgive me because I was a fool.

A total and utter fool to push her away.

That thought hit me upside the damn head at the exact moment that stun gun took me down. Maybe the jolt cleared my head and I should be thankful. I don't know. All I do know is no one better hurt my girl. I'm coming for her and whoever gets in my way is as good as dead.

I pray to God I get to Carlotta in time because there's no doubt in my mind that she's in serious trouble. Gallo fucked up once and lost his chance because I stepped in and rescued her. That means he's going to be extra careful and diligent this time around. He isn't going to stop until he snuffs out her beautiful light and I refuse to let that happen.

No fucking way.

My muscles begin to respond as the stun wears off and I sit up and pull my phone out of my jacket. With shaking hands, I call Miceli's number.

"Archer," he says in answer. "Is she on the plane?"

"Not exactly." *Shit.* I hate having to tell her brother that I screwed up. "We got to her place and less than five minutes later, some of Gallo's guys broke down the door."

Miceli swears.

"They hit me with a stun gun and took her. We need to find her and fast."

"Any idea where they went?" Miceli is all business and ready to roll which I appreciate.

"No, but I can reach out to my contacts."

"Put an obscene reward up for any information that leads to my sister."

"Roger that."

"In the meantime, come over to my place. I'll call my brothers."

"Yeah, on my way. And Miceli..." My voice trails off. Christ, I feel awful. If anything happens to Carlotta...

Shit. I can't even let my brain go there.

"What?"

"I'm sorry. We should've gone straight to the airport. I should've known better."

"It's not your fault. I said to take her back to her apartment so she could pack a bag. If anything, this is my fault."

"We're going to get her back," I tell him, my voice filled with conviction.

"Call your contacts, Archer. Then get your ass over here."

"Roger."

We disconnect and I immediately leave the apartment and head back down to my car. They're long gone by now and the only way I'm going to find Carlotta is by hoping and praying one of my informants comes through with a good lead. And fast because time is running out.

Once I'm seated in my Challenger, I pull up an encrypted message and send it out to everyone I have on my roster. Of course, I also make sure to mention Miceli Rossi's name and how he's offering a huge financial incentive for any intel that leads to his sister. After sending the message, I start my car and turn it toward Billionaire's Row where Miceli and Alessia reside.

His sister.

The words hit me hard because not only did I fuck up by letting Carlotta get taken, I also messed up royally by sleeping with her and then telling her my insensitive demands about whatever happens stays up at the cabin, yadda, yadda, yadda.

God, I feel like an utter ass. She was a virgin and gave me her body and, I think, a little piece of her heart. And what do I do? Toss it back in her face and repeatedly say I can't be with her because my lifestyle is too dangerous.

Yes, that's true. Well, partly. I lead a dangerous life and I never want to put her in a precarious position. But what just happened has nothing to do with me or what I do for a living in the shadows. Carmine Gallo is bound and determined to plant his fat ass at the table with the Five Families. In order to do that, he plans on doing whatever it takes to usurp the Rossi family's seat.

Even if I wasn't in the picture, Carlotta would still be in danger. But because I am involved, now her chances of being found that much faster have increased. So it's a good thing I'm in her life, right?

"Fucking right," I grumble. Finding Carlotta and returning her safely to her family is my number one priority. And maybe, just maybe, me being in her life isn't a bad thing. If I'm with her then she's always going to be protected and taken care of and…loved.

My heart does a weird little dip at the thought. I've never been in love before, so I can't say for sure, but I think I am damn close to being in love with Carloota…if I'm not already there. Vulnerability is something I've always avoided because I thought it made a man look weak. But I'm learning that having such strong feelings for Carlotta doesn't make me feel weak at all.

The issue with Caitlin is I wasn't there—emotionally and, most of the time, physically, too. Of course, realistically, no two people can always be together twenty-four hours a day. But, for the first time, I'm beginning to realize having me around isn't necessarily a bad thing. I have contacts, I have skills and, most importantly, I have the experience necessary to do whatever it takes. And with zero regrets.

Traffic is a pain in the ass, as usual, but I don't let it slow me down. I know I'm driving too fast, being reckless, but Carlotta's life is on the line. I'm almost to Miceli's place when the worst thought in the world hits me.

What if we can't save her? What if I lose Carlotta?

The idea of Gallo killing her makes my gut clench and churn. She's so sweet, so good, so innocent. I can't let her become collateral damage like Caitlin. Suddenly, worst case scenarios start bombarding me like shrapnel. What if none of my contacts come through? What if we're too late and, just like Caitlin, I walk into a room somewhere and find Carlotta's lifeless body on the floor, blood pouring from her mortal wounds and soaking the floor?

"Fuck." I push my foot harder against the accelerator and swerve around a car stopped at a four-way stop sign and blow through the intersection after a cursory glance. I don't have time to stop or yield or wait around, and I can feel each precious second draining away like the sands in an hourglass.

And that fucking terrifies me.

Doing my best to stay focused, I suppress the biting panic threatening to make me go into a tailspin. It's important, now more than ever, to stay level headed and be prepared, both mentally and physically.

"Get a grip, Archer," I scold myself. "You're no good and can't help her if you panic."

In all my years of ghost ops, I never panicked. Not once. I've always remained calm, cool and collected under pressure. But the idea of losing Carlotta is making me a little crazy and a lot worried.

Yes, we had sex, but it was so much more than that. Thinking back over our brief time together at the cabin makes my heart squeeze painfully. I'm not sure when or how, but that little firecracker cast a spell over me. She charmed me into feeling things I've never felt before and now all I want to do is wrap my arms around her and keep her safe.

Unfortunately, I can't do that. Not yet, anyway. Instead, I'm trapped in some horrible waiting game, not knowing the consequences of what's going to happen, and it's killing me.

After what feels like forever, I pull up into the visitor parking spot at Miceli's building and jump out of the car. Once I'm inside the tall, extravagant building, I hop in the elevator and it zooms me straight up to his floor.

Heart in my throat and clinging to my phone like a lifeline, I knock on the door and it's immediately opened.

"Archer, come on in. Have you heard anything yet?" Miceli asks, brow furrowed and gaze intense as he closes the door behind me. I can see the worry in every line on his face and I wish I had better news to deliver, but my contacts haven't responded yet. It's barely been twenty minutes, though, so that's not unusual. Just frustrating as hell.

"Not yet," I say. "Hopefully very soon."

He motions for me to follow him into the living room where his brothers and their wives are gathered, along with Leo Amato, his bodyguard and best friend, and his woman Gia DeLucca, Alessia's older sister. Everyone looks so serious and glum. It fucking shreds my heart. I'm blaming myself, wishing I could've done more and stopped those assholes. But I can't focus on that because what if's and could have's aren't going to help Carlotta right now. I have to remain positive and we need to come together and do whatever it takes to get my girl back.

Because, yeah, she's mine. There's no point denying it. I'm falling or maybe I've already fallen. To be honest, I don't know what the fuck is going on. My heart is in a turmoil and these feelings she's stirred up inside of me are all so new. Whatever the case, I need Carlotta Rossi like I've never needed anyone before.

I need my girl like the very air I'm breathing.

The realization clobbers my normally cool heart like a sledgehammer and a fire begins to burn inside my veins. I'll do anything to find her. Even if that means putting myself in danger or sacrificing my life in order to save hers.

I've always been a protector and a warrior, and I've sacrificed a lot for my country. But this is extremely personal. It's not just business as usual. If this rescue mission goes up in flames and ends in disaster, I will never get over it. The guilt will be my undoing and losing Carlotta means I will lose myself, too. And this time there won't be any coming back.

I can't sit around and continue to do nothing or I'll go out of my blasted mind. We need to come up with a plan. We need to find her. Leaning against the wall, I cross my arms as her brothers begin to ask a million questions about what happened at her place.

I fill them in as quickly and thoroughly as I can. There's not a lot to share because I was down and out for most of the time. But I tell them three armed men broke the door down and when I rushed into the living room, they were waiting for me.

"I told Carlotta to hide, but your sister doesn't exactly listen very well," I say, my tone dry.

"Who? Lottie?" Angelo makes a mock-confused face. "You're kidding, right?"

"She's definitely a firecracker," I murmur, picturing the cute way her face pinches and her nose scrunches right before she goes all ballistic about something.

"Ah, so you've witnessed Carlotta the Crusher?" Vin asks wryly.

I snort back a laugh. "That's a fitting nickname."

"Yeah, our baby sis can crush the biggest balls with ease," Enzo states.

"She sure can," I murmur. My heart clenches with emotion and I look down at my phone's screen, willing a text to appear with information about Carlotta's whereabouts. Fuck, any lead at this point will be something.

Heaving out a frustrated breath, I rake a hand through my hair then look back up and realize everyone is staring at me. Her brothers have curious expressions on their faces while their wives exchange knowing smiles.

I'm not sure when I became so easily readable, but I do my best to mask any expression from my face. No one needs to know what happened between Carlotta and I up at the cabin. Hell, it wouldn't end well for me if four Rossi men want to kill me for touching their baby sister.

"Okay, everyone," Miceli says, clearing his throat and taking charge of the room. "Let's go over exactly what we know and what we're going to do about getting Lottie back. Because if Archer's contacts don't come through, we're still moving."

Miceli Rossi is larger than life, the biggest physically out of all of us, and he commandeers a room and captivates an audience like no one else. It's why he's able to lead the Five Families so well. People look to him for guidance and he is respected by so many important leaders and businessmen in this city.

However, Carmine Gallo is not one of them. And he's going down.

Because the alternative would be to let him win and there's no way in hell we can let that happen. He's evil personified and his agenda to take over the table can't be good.

While Carlotta's family discusses every single angle and possible option we have—and without intel there isn't much—I mentally will my contacts to pull through. A sick feeling eats away at my stomach lining like a bad ulcer. If we don't get to Carlotta soon, I'm terrified that she is going to suffer the same fate as Caitlin. And if that happens, I will never forgive myself.

17

CARLOTTA

I'm bouncing around in the back seat of an SUV and I have no idea where we're headed, but I'd be willing to bet my last dollar I'll be seeing Carmine Gallo's ugly mug very soon. I'm more worried about Damon, though. In my head, I've been thanking every angel above since we left my apartment building that they didn't turn their guns on him.

I can still picture him lying there on the floor, completely helpless and at their mercy. God, it kills me to think about what could have happened. My only agenda was getting these three thugs out of there before they decided to do something stupid. Before they decided to kill Damon.

Releasing a shaky breath, it occurs to me that I would've done anything to keep him safe. Even if that would've meant being reckless and throwing myself in front of a bullet for him. And, yes, it's crazy because we haven't even known each other for very long, but no matter what Damon thinks about himself, I know he's a good man. Besides, after he rescued me, I figure I owe him one.

We drive for what feels like forever, but it is probably only twenty minutes or so. I'm beginning to grow anxious and I know escaping is going to be harder this time around because Gallo will be better prepared. Granted, I had some help last time thanks to Damon, but I have the sinking feeling I'm very much on my own this time around.

How could I not be? No one has any idea where I am, including me. That's going to make it extremely difficult for my brothers and Damon to swoop in and save me.

So it looks like I'm going to have to save myself. I just have to be smarter than Gallo. And, truthfully, I don't think that's going to be that big of a challenge. The man is so power hungry that he makes mistakes right and left. Instead of being smooth and sneaky, he barrels into town with a clear and obvious agenda, provoking my family and causing problems. That makes me think he isn't all that bright. Or he's just so blinded by what he wants—power and control over NYC's mafia families—that he's tripping up and being foolhardy, brash and far too impulsive for his own good.

And that all works in my favor. The second he slips, I'm going to take immediate advantage of the situation. Whether that means securing a weapon and battling my way out or it means getting free and running, I'll be prepared to take action.

Clenching my fists, I keep my attention on the passing scenery outside, searching for landmarks and trying to pinpoint our exact location. I don't have my cell phone so I can't call my brothers, but I might be able to communicate my whereabouts at some point, if I escape Gallo.

Correction—when I escape Gallo.

Stay positive, I tell myself. My family can't let a power hungry, mad man like Carmine Gallo win. No freaking way.

And knowing my brothers like I do, I can guarantee Gallo's days in NYC are numbered.

We left the city and drove off the expressway a little bit ago. After driving along a rural road for maybe another ten minutes, the driver turns the SUV down a dirt drive. We pass through some tall trees, the tires crunching over gravel, and a farm house comes into view. It's large and cozy-looking with a wraparound porch. The kind of place I could picture in a Hallmark movie. Except I know better. The evil lurking inside it would never be found in a feel-good film starring Candace Cameron Bure. Nope, more like a Stephen King flick.

Just beyond the house, I catch a glimpse of a barn. I'm expecting to stop in the front driveway, but we continue around back and pull to a stop in front of the barn. It doesn't look nearly as nice as the house in front and I start getting creepy vibes, a tingle erupting at the base of my neck.

The SUV doors open and, a second later, I'm being yanked out. My feet hit the ground with a thud and I try to dig my heels in, but it's useless. The big thug has my arm locked in a bone-crunching hold and I have no choice except to follow along with his fast, clipped pace.

One of the other men swings the barn door open and we go inside. It's gloomy and the smell of hay fills my nose. There's also a musty smell permeating the air and I have a feeling there haven't been any animals living in here for a very long time. No equipment hangs from the walls and the horse stalls are empty. Not even one chicken in sight. Although, I can't exactly picture Carmine Gallo dressed in overalls and playing farmer. Maybe this place belongs to someone else. Seems like it's been deserted for a while.

"We meet again."

My head snaps over to see Gallo stroll in through a side door and he's looking just as smug as I remember. God, I hate this guy.

"You may have escaped me once, Ms. Rossi, but I can assure you that will not be happening again."

"We'll see," I say, an edge of challenge in my voice. Because if he thinks I'm just going to lay down and give in, that I'm not going to fight him every step of the way, he must be forgetting I have Rossi blood flowing through my veins.

His dark eyes narrow and I do everything to keep myself from spitting at him. How dare he think he can target and destroy my family. We've done nothing to provoke him.

"Take her up," he orders.

Up? For a moment, I'm confused because I didn't see an upstairs, but as the big thug roughly guides me toward the rear of the barn, I notice a loft. It's pretty high, maybe twenty feet up, and I'm shoved against the ladder.

"Go," the huge jerk orders, and I bristle. I hate being ordered around. Especially by big brutish men with no manners and who work for an asshole like Carmine Gallo.

But I have to be smart about this and play my cards right. Ideally, I'd like to lull Gallo into a false sense of security, make him think I'm just a stupid, harmless woman with no agenda. And then I'll strike when he least expects it.

Letting out a breath, I tilt my head back and look up into the darkness. Not good. My heart starts thumping harder and I wonder why he wants me to go up into the loft. I have a feeling nothing good can come of this, but what choice do I have?

I briefly squeeze my eyes shut then force myself to grab onto a rung, step up and begin to climb. I'm not scared of heights, but once I'm on the second level, my pulse kicks up as I look over the barn below. I have a bird's eye view of the entire first floor, and it's awfully high and more than a little intimidating.

Stepping away from the edge, I glance around and don't see much other than a hay-strewn floor, some bales of hay that are stacked up, and large, wooden beams crisscrossing above me.

Why am I up here? I wonder. I have no idea what he's up to or planning, but I know it can't be good.

As if in answer, Gallo appears, steps over the edge and sends me an evil smile. I mentally warn myself not to underestimate the man. Everything in me is screaming he's a fool, but he's a dangerous and possibly deranged fool, and that's a very bad combination.

Even though I know I should be scared, I'm more pissed off than anything. Especially because he's out to ruin the people I love most in this whole world. And that can't happen. No way. Not on my watch.

Turning to face my kidnapper, I toss my hair over my shoulder and place my hands on my hips. "What the hell do you want from my family? We haven't done anything to you." I make sure my voice stays firm and strong. The last thing I want to do is show any fear because that's like blood in the water to a shark like Gallo. If he smells my fear, he will strike and try to take me out.

"You haven't done anything to me?" he echoes. A short, harsh laugh erupts from his throat. "That isn't exactly true, Ms. Rossi."

He vehemently spits my name out with such caustic hate that I nearly cringe. It's like acid drips from his tongue and I wisely decide it's time to tread lightly because he's clearly harboring a huge vendetta. Maybe even bigger than I realized.

But why? There has to be more to the story than the few details that I already know.

"Your brother's wife sicced assassins and bounty hunters on me."

Well, tit for tat, I think, but I keep my mouth shut. If the bastard wouldn't have put Angelo and Blake's names on the Kill List then that wouldn't have happened. She just managed to flip the tables on him and now he's mad.

"Then they all descended on my mansion and a war broke out, burning it down to the ground. I barely escaped with my life."

I stifle the urge to sigh. This isn't new information and I wonder how much longer he's going to cry about it. As far as I'm concerned, if this is his reason for wanting to destroy my family, it's a piss-poor reason. Especially since he started it.

"All I wanted was a chance to sit among the mafia greats in this city. It's what I deserve," he seethes.

Yeah, yeah. Maybe this really is just about him wanting more power. My gut thought there might be more to it, but maybe I'm wrong. Perhaps Carmine Gallo is just a power-hungry man who wants to exert his dominance over everyone else. I suppose it's really nothing new and happens all the time. If I had a dollar for every person who tried to topple the top players in New York City and take over, I'd have a fortune.

"It's more than that, though," he says in a voice so low, I almost don't understand him. But he's definitely caught my attention and I find myself perking up.

What in the world is he talking about?

"It's what I'm owed," he continues, voice full of fury, "and I will collect what is my due."

A frown creases my brow. "I have no idea what you're talking about. No one owes you anything—"

"The Rossi's owe me my son back!" he yells, and I flinch. Completely startled by his outburst, I take a wary step back. "It's because of your family that he's dead!"

He's breathing hard, his face a mottled shade of reddish-purple, and he's clenching and unclenching his fists. I'm not following him, but he has my full and undivided attention. The last thing I want to do is aggravate him or piss him off further, but I need to know what it is he's talking about.

"I don't know what you're talking about," I say again softly.

He sends me a glare that should make me tremble. But, honestly, I'm more curious than scared or intimidated.

"Of course, you don't! Carlotta Rossi has no idea what's going on, does she? She's just the sweet, innocent little sister who doesn't get too involved in her family's business affairs. Poor, clueless Lottie," he sneers, taking a step closer.

I hold my ground, but do a quick sweep for a weapon, searching for anything I could grab and use against him. Only one of the thugs is up here with us, so it might be possible to take him or Gallo down. Unfortunately, I don't see anything useful.

"It's so much easier that way, isn't it? Not knowing? It lets you sleep in your big bed every night with no guilt or regrets, huh? Well, wake the fuck up, little girl! Because your family is nothing but a bunch of murdering, money-grubbing assholes! And they will pay—they all will…starting with you."

"Wait!" I hold up a hand when he lurches forward. "If you tell me what happened, maybe I can help you. Maybe we can fix whatever the problem is and—"

"You can't fix dead," he states flatly. "And your family killed my boy."

My eyes widen. I did not expect him to say that. "What are you talking about?"

I do my best to sound concerned, sympathetic even.

But he doesn't answer my question and, instead, he motions to his thug. "Help me. Grab the rope."

Without hesitation, the big guy retrieves a coil of rope from the dim corner of the loft. He tosses it up and over one of the big wooden beams and I get a sinking feeling in my stomach. This doesn't look good and I turn around, trying to figure out how I can escape this mess.

A hand tightens around my arm and yanks me forward. "No, you're not going anywhere," Gallo says. "Give me the rope. And hold her."

Shit. While his henchman holds me tightly in his iron grip, Gallo tosses the rope around my neck. A noose. *Oh, my God.* Panic flares up inside me and I struggle, trying to break free, but then the rope is pulled tighter and I freeze as I'm pulled up onto my toes.

No, no, no. I don't want to die like this. My mind turns to Damon and all the things I never had a chance to say to him. The idea of never being able to kiss him or touch him again makes me want to cry and scream and lash out. But I can barely move.

"Let me tell you a little story," Gallo says in a low voice, moving closer. Until we're eye to eye. "I used to have a son your age. He would've been twenty-five this month, actually. But now he's six-feet under, thanks to your family."

The rope is cutting into my throat, making it hard to breathe, and I don't dare try to talk. I can barely move my head. My eyes can move, but my neck is securely bound, forced to face forward. Drawing in a ragged breath, all I can do is wait for Gallo to continue.

"Maximo, my son, worked for a company that ran into some hard times. He owed a lot of people money and became worried. People come after you in this town…when you owe them enough money. But the owner told him everything would be fine—that the Rossi family was going to acquire and save his floundering company. Everything had been set up, and the paperwork was ready to be signed."

His story is starting to sound very familiar all too fast. But I'm still not sure how he can blame my family if the deal didn't go through. Because I have a pretty good feeling this is connected to Holloway Corp. and Enzo and Gabriella.

A moment later, Gallo confirms my suspicions.

"When Enzo abruptly backed out of the deal, it was up to Gabriella Bianche to help. After all, she was the one who'd originally expressed interest in buying the company. And then she backed out for no apparent reason."

That's not true, I think. Both Enzo and Gabriella decided against acquiring Doug Holloway's company because he turned out to be a liar and a pig. He'd pitted them against each other and played games with their heads. And their hearts. Luckily, they'd discovered who Holloway really was and they'd both rescinded their initial offers to obtain his failing company.

"It's not up to my family to save every struggling business," I tell him. "If Holloway mismanaged funds, how is that our fault?"

"Because they could've saved it which in turn would've saved my son!" he practically screams at me.

I flinch and his face is right in front of mine. I've never seen someone so full of rage and hate. It's oozing off of him in clumps.

"I'm sorry if your son had to find a new job—"

"He didn't find a new job! He left a note saying he was a failure and couldn't pay off his debts. Then he threw himself off the nearest bridge."

Oh, God.

"So instead of hiding or waiting to be killed because he owed the wrong people money—or asking me for help because he didn't want to be a burden—he ended his life."

It takes me a few seconds to soak in what he's saying—the significance of losing a child, why he blames my family and what that currently means for me at this moment.

Nothing good.

"I'm sorry about your son," I say quietly, and I truly am. "But I can guarantee Enzo and Gabriella had no idea or they would've helped."

But it's like he doesn't even hear me. Or doesn't want to.

"Now you see why I have to destroy your family," he says. "Because the Rossi's are the reason my son is dead."

Talk about faulty logic. I understand the connection he's making, but what happened was a tragedy and shouldn't solely land on my family's shoulders. Because I know for an absolute fact that if Enzo and Gabriella knew Gallo's son was that desperate, they could have and would have helped him find a new job elsewhere.

But Gallo clearly believes that my family is responsible for his son's death and I don't think there's any way to make him see the truth or be logical. His emotions are ruling his decisions right now. He only sees what he wants to see—that we're one-hundred percent at fault for what happened.

"I'm going to eliminate every last one of you and then take your place as part of the ruling Five Families. And then I'm going to bring the whole table down. After all, Gabriella was a Bianche, so they need to go, too."

I think Gallo has officially lost his mind.

"So let's send your brothers a little video, shall we?" There's a taunting tone to his voice that sets my nerves on edge and puts fear in my heart. I have no idea what he's planning and I'm pretty sure that I don't want to know either.

Unable to move, I squeeze my eyes, praying to wake up from this nightmare. When I open them again, I see him pull out his phone. My heart thunders and I immediately try to shake my head, but I can't because of the rope around my neck. I don't want my brothers or Damon to see me like this. They're going to flip out.

"Why?" I croak. "What's the point?"

If he's going to kill me, the last thing I want him to do is film it. Feeling sick to my stomach, I whimper, unable to move. I've never felt so helpless in my entire life. If this is it, if I'm going to die, I don't want him to send a horrible video of my death to my family. It would devastate them.

Unfortunately, I have no say or control over the situation. When Gallo hits record, I do my best not to cry. And I fail miserably.

18

ARCHER

Carlotta's brothers, their wives and I have done our best to talk out the situation and come up with a tentative game plan while I wait for some kind of a lead to come in from one of my contacts. I've received a few calls, but nothing useful. The vague, very general leads—like someone saw a black SUV—isn't going to help us find Lottie. Good to know, sure, but I'm still pacing like a lunatic because I've never felt so damned helpless in my entire life.

Meanwhile, Miceli touched base with the other four mafia families. They've vowed to help and are ready to move the moment we call. And that makes me feel good. I'm surprised at how easily they came together and how ready they are to go to war for one another. But the group who sits at the table has evolved over the past year. All of the troublemakers are gone and the ones who currently rule are loyal as hell. And that's a great thing for us right now. The last thing I want is for anyone to stall or drag their feet. All hands are on deck and I couldn't be more grateful.

But, time seems to be dragging by and I can't stop pacing, my phone is radio silent, and I'm on the verge of losing my shit. The urge to move fills me and if we don't do something soon, I'm going to implode.

Hell, I'll burn this city to the ground if that's what it takes to find Carlotta.

Suddenly, everyone's phone seems to ding or buzz with a text at once. We all open up our messages at the same time and I see it's from an unknown caller.

"All from unknown?" Miceli asks, and Vin, Enzo, Angelo and I confirm yes.

"It's a video," Vin states, and the women gather round to see their husband's screens.

"Yeah, I have a bad feeling about this," Angelo says. Blake wraps an arm around his waist, her attention on his phone.

I hit play and an extremely close-up image of Carlotta fills my screen. Her pretty brown eyes shine with tears and my stomach twists.

"What the fuck is this?" I hiss, hating the fear I see in her brown gaze. I swear to God, I am one step away from losing my shit. I wish I could jump through my phone's screen and save her from whatever has her in an icy grip of fear. Because I would kill whoever made her cry. I'd kill them with my bare hands and then empty my entire gun in them for good measure.

As if on cue, the camera slowly pulls back and I get my first look at the noose around her neck. My stomach sinks and my grip tightens so hard around my phone's case, I hear it crack.

"Oh, my God," Alessia whispers. Hannah gasps and Gabriella and Blake grimace.

"As you can all see, your sister is in a world of trouble," a voice says and I want to punch my fist through the screen. "You might say she's hanging on by a thread…or a rope."

"Fucking Gallo," Miceli growls.

Gallo laughs and a chill runs down my spine. Carmine Gallo has lost his fucking mind. And poor Carlotta is at the receiving end of his insane bullshit.

How could I have let this happen? I never should've taken her back to her apartment. A little voice in my head had warned me, but I ignored it. I figured we'd be in and out in under ten minutes. Well, I guess that's all it fucking took to lose the woman who was quickly becoming so damn important to me.

I don't care what anyone else says, this is all my fault. I should've listened to my gut. Feeling sick, I watch the rest of the video play out and it only gets worse.

"I'm not sure if you can see," Gallo continues smugly, "but right below your dear sister's feet are standing on a trap door." He uses his foot to brush the hay away, revealing a door in the loft's floor.

Several curses fill the air. I swallow down the vomit creeping up the back of my throat.

No. Carlotta is so innocent, so good, so sweet. Gallo is a fucking monster for doing this to her and I'm going to fucking kill him. If it's the last thing I do, I'm going to put him in the ground.

"I've rigged the door to drop in exactly one hour. Oh, no wait. Maybe I only set it for forty-five minutes." He laughs again and my skin crawls. "No matter. Either way, when the trap door opens, Carlotta drops and the rope will tighten. I doubt that you have enough time to prevent that, but I wanted to prepare you for what you'll find—your baby sister's corpse swinging from the rafters."

"That sick sonofabitch," Angelo grates out.

"Where the fuck is she?" Vin asks, raking a hand through his air.

"I have a funny feeling he's about to tell us," Enzo says, his dark eyes glued to his screen.

Miceli's nostrils flare. "And then we kill him."

I lock eyes with Miceli and nod. "I'm going to rip his fucking heart out," I growl. "Then string him up."

I can't get my hands around Gallo's throat fast enough. Maybe I'll wring the life out of him before I hang him. There are so many ways I could kill him, but none of them seem good enough. Whatever I do, though, I'm going to do it with a smile on my face.

White-hot anger floods through me as Gallo continues to taunt us and waste precious time. After what feels like forever, but has probably only been about a minute, he finally starts getting to the point.

"I want you to come here, so I can continue destroying your family, one by one. I'm not scared of you—not one of you—and I'm ready."

"What the fuck did we ever do to this guy?" Enzo asks, completely bewildered like the rest of us.

As if in answer, Gallo looks directly into the camera and says, "You took something from me and now I'm going to take *everything* from you. Starting with your baby sister."

Click. The video ends and, a few seconds later, all of our phones receive a text from him, revealing his location.

Bingo! He's so overly-confident and believes he can beat us. No way. Yes, he's luring us into a trap, but we're not stupid. I used to do this kind of shit all the time. I've snuck into enemy war zones and rescued hostages without ever having been seen. I was a damn good Delta operator. So good that my middle fucking name may as well be stealth.

So if Carmine Gallo thinks he has any kind of a chance against me, he's sorely mistaken. He's just taunted the wrong fucking man because I am going to take him out before he even knows what hit him. Just like my team used to do. Operation: Sagittarius is a go and fucking heads are about to roll.

The five of us bolt into action. Words are rapid-fire exchanged, and the women step back after quickly kissing their respective men. Without a second to spare, I race over to the elevator and slam my palm on the down button, Carlotta's brothers right on my heels. This is it and we all know it. Failure is not an option.

Carlotta's life literally hangs in the balance.

We'd already talked over what we'd do the moment we discovered Carlotta's location and as soon as the elevator reaches the garage and opens, I'm running over to Miceli's SUV along with Leo Amato, while Enzo, Vin and Angelo make their way to Blake's Jeep. It's good for off-road driving and we figured it might be better than driving one of their more sporty cars. It's best to be prepared because who knows what kind of terrain we might encounter.

The three of us are barely situated in Miceli's SUV before he's backing it up and zooming toward the exit. I pull up the GPS on my phone and plug in the location that Gallo gave us, waiting impatiently for the directions to pop up.

We're all under the assumption that this is a trap, that he's trying to lure us to our own destruction like he said, so we have every intention of being careful. The only reason Gallo revealed his location is because he's waiting and he's ready.

But, so are we. Enzo should've placed the call to the other four mafia families by now. They are on stand-by, waiting to hear from him, and now they should be moving. We have backup and I gotta say, I have full confidence in the dangerous men coming to our aid.

We just need to make sure we get there in time. If we don't...

Fuck. I can't even think about it. There's no choice but to save Carlotta and defeat Gallo.

"ETA?" Miceli barks, all business, eyes glued to the road. He drives like a bat out of hell, and I lay a hand against the dashboard as he expertly maneuvers the vehicle around other traffic and through intersections.

"Thirty minutes," I reply grimly.

"I'll get us there in fifteen," he states confidently and floors it. The Range Rover squeals around a bus and I realize I'm holding my breath. Not because of Miceli's driving, but because I can't stop picturing Carlotta's face in that goddamn video. I could tell she was trying to be incredibly brave, but I saw the fear in her pretty brown eyes.

And the tears. Even though the video was slightly grainy, I couldn't miss the bright tears glistening in her dark eyes and it makes my heart break. I'm not sure when my heart became capable of loving again, not exactly aware of the exact moment it flooded with warmth and life again, but I have an idea.

It was the moment Carlotta Rossi swept into my life dressed up like the Queen of Hearts. She's truly the loveliest creature I've ever met, and it's so much more than her beauty. More than the sex, too. As good as that was, it's Carlotta's warmth and smile and goodness that draws me to her, that makes me want to lose myself in her and absorb some of the amazing light she radiates.

The truth is I'm falling so hard for her, it feels like I've been run over by a semi truck. Getting to her in time, saving her before the trap door drops, is going to happen. We're going to beat Gallo at his own game because there's no other alternative.

I plan to ride off into the sunset with my woman. I just hope Gallo, or her brothers, don't murder me beforehand.

Glancing over at Miceli, his jaw set and determined, I wonder if he'd approve of me with his sister. *Shit.* I honestly don't know what he's going to do when he finds out. But, one thing at a time. First, we have to save Lottie.

Then I face her brothers and tell them the truth—I love their little sister.

My phone vibrates and I look down to see a text from Enzo. I read it fast then look over at Miceli and then over the backseat at Leo. "The other families all confirmed. Our plan is moving forward and all the players know what to do."

Miceli gives me a sharp nod and then yanks the wheel, careening off the expressway. He said he'd get us there in fifteen minutes, but I think it's going to be even less than that. The man is driving like he's in the Daytona 500 and that's just fine with me.

"Alright, we're going to try this the easy way first," Miceli says and stabs a finger against his cell phone. He's calling Gallo and with each ring of the phone, my heart beats a little harder.

Right before the call drops into voicemail, Gallo picks up. "Did you get my video?" he asks coolly. I can hear the smile in his voice and it makes me want to throttle him to within an inch of his life...and then put a bullet between his beady eyes. Forcing myself to keep it together, I look over at Miceli who is trying equally hard to remain calm and not explode.

But we know we have to keep it together right now...for Carlotta. So the best thing to do is not take the bait.

"The Five Families have reconsidered and would like to discuss you becoming a member of the table...if you return Carlotta safely."

If Gallo agrees then this all ends now. That seems far too easy and his next words prove exactly what I'm thinking—that Carmine Gallo wants more than just a seat at the table. He wants to destroy the Five Families completely.

"Too little, too late. That time has passed and I'm no longer interested. But thank you for the generous offer." His voice oozes with sarcasm.

Well, so much for the easy way.

"Why don't you think about it before dismissing it so easily," Miceli says, trying to buy us more time.

"There's nothing to think about!" Gallo snaps. "I'd rather kill you all."

The hatred in his voice is pure evil and there has to be something deeper going on here. I just have no idea what. Before Miceli can even respond, Gallo hangs up.

"So much for that," Leo grumbles from the back seat.

"He's dead," Miceli growls.

"There has to be more to this than simply wanting a seat at the table," I muse, thinking out loud. "Gallo is filled with such vicious hate and he's so hellbent on destroying your entire family…"

My voice trails off as they contemplate my words.

"I agree," Leo says. "This has to run deeper."

Miceli lets out a frustrated sound. "If it does—and I agree with you—I have no idea what it could possibly be. But, yeah, it definitely feels personal and I don't know why."

"Whatever it is, it doesn't matter. The only thing that matters is rescuing Lottie," I say, sounding more passionate than I intend.

Miceli slants me a side glance. "When did you start calling her Lottie?"

Even though his voice is merely filled with curiosity, I feel my entire body tense. "At the cabin," I tell him carefully, shifting uneasily in my seat.

I glance back at Leo and see his smirk. *Bastard.* He always was extremely perceptive.

Instead of commenting further, Miceli checks the GPS then hits the brakes.

"We're here," he states. "Everyone ready?"

I lay my hand over the gun in my holster and nod. "Let's go get Carlotta."

Time to go in guns blazing.

19

CARLOTTA

I'm going to die.

As hard as I'm trying to be positive, the reality of my situation is bleak. Standing up on my tiptoes hurts now, but if I try to lower myself down further on my feet, the rope cuts into my neck. The knowledge that I'm standing on a trap door rigged to open soon sends another tear running down my face.

How the hell am I supposed to get out of this awful situation? It's impossible. Maybe accepting my fate with dignity and peace is all I can do.

Except that's not me. I'm a fighter to my core and I always have been. Just rolling over and accepting defeat isn't how I operate. Survival is ingrained in my very DNA and now isn't the time to turn into a quitter. Now is when I need to step up and dig deeper than I ever have before. And that starts with being brave and smart.

Because I have a reason and his name is Damon Archer. No matter what he says, I know he cares. I know it, can feel it, on a soul level. There's a reason he pulls away and claims he can't get too involved. He thinks he failed his past girlfriend and blames himself for Cailin's death. But that was a tragic situation and certainly not his fault. I don't blame him for what happened and he certainly shouldn't blame himself. I hate how the guilt of that relationship has made him think he can't have another relationship. It breaks my heart because he is a good man, deserving and worthy of love. I need to reassure him in me, in us, in a future together.

But first, I need to get the hell out of here.

After filming me, Gallo left and I have no idea where he went. He even took his big thug with him, so I'm all alone now. This could be my one and only chance to try to escape and I don't want to waste it.

My hands aren't bound and I've been clutching at the rope wound around my neck, trying to loosen it, but having no success. So what else can I do?

Think, Lottie.

Chewing on my lower lip, I try to slip my fingers between my skin and the rope, but it's too damn tight. It's forcing my chin up and my gaze flits up to the rafters above me where the rope is looped. If only I could saw through it. God, I'd give anything for a knife right now.

It's hard to look directly down because of the way I'm positioned, so I can't see my feet at all. I didn't even know there was a trap door beneath me until that bastard Gallo callously announced it while he was filming his freaking video.

God, I feel like I'm in one of those awful underground and very illegal films where they kill the poor, unsuspecting person. I don't want to be a victim. And I certainly don't want to go out this way, for these to be my final moments.

Twisting my body, I tell myself to remain calm, but the truth is all my logic is draining out of my body and panic is starting to consume me. I can feel the hope I was trying desperately to maintain earlier slowly slipping away.

Suddenly, I'm so damn angry—at my situation, at my helplessness and, most of all, at that last conversation Damon and I had in the car.

"We agreed once we went back to the city, you and I would go our separate ways."

"I know what you said, but it's not what I want. I think we owe it to each other to explore whatever this is more fully."

"No. It's impossible. You're leaving and I already told you I can't do that."

"Why? Because of what happened with Caitlin? This is totally different—"

"I don't want a relationship with you, Carlotta. I can't. I'm sorry. I thought I made that clear."

Letting things end that way hurts my heart on the deepest level. We shared something so special—from the first moment we met at the masquerade party—and now it's all going to end far too soon and beyond tragically.

Even though my throat is encased with rope, a sob manages to slip out. I give myself exactly one minute to lose my shit and cry my eyes out. To be sad and hopeless and have a pity party. Once I let myself mourn the way everything went so horribly wrong, after I get the emotions all out, I pull in a sharp breath, wipe the snot away dripping from my nose and decide to figure out my escape.

Because I am not some helpless princess waiting for her knight in shining armor to come rescue her. I am a strong, smart, fierce woman and I can do this.

I *have* to do this. At this point, the alternative is death and I am not ready to die. Despite what Damon said, I believe we still might have a chance. Yes, the odds are stacked against me, but it's time to make my move. And, hopefully, it will end up being a power move that changes the outcome of the game.

Sending up a silent prayer, I think back to the video and what Gallo said.

"I'm not sure if you can see, but right below your dear sister's feet is a trap door."

He'd brushed some hay aside to reveal the door beneath my feet.

"I've rigged the door to drop in exactly one hour. Oh, no wait. Maybe I only set it for forty-five minutes. No matter. Either way, when the trap door opens, Carlotta drops and the rope will tighten. I'm not sure you have enough time to prevent that, but I wanted to prepare you for what you'll find—your baby sister's corpse swinging from the rafters."

Yeah, we'll see about that, asshole, I think. But, I'm wondering where the timer is that's supposedly counting down my imminent demise. At this point, it's been over thirty minutes since he filmed the video. Maybe closer to forty minutes and that's damn scary if what he said is true. Either way, I'm closing in on the forty-five minute mark fast. And that can't be good.

I do my best to look around and find the timer. If I can stop it then the door won't trigger open in the next five to fifteen minutes. At least that will give me some more time, a bit of wiggle room, and a chance to figure my way out of this awful situation.

And then I spot it, up in the rafters, and my heart sinks. The red glowing numerals show less than ten minutes and the seconds are disappearing so fast that I feel a sick twist in my gut. There is absolutely no way in hell I can reach that. Despite the utter futility of it, I reach up, my hand straining for an object that's completely out of my reach.

Oh, God. I'm going to die in less than ten minutes.

And what do I have to show for it? Not much, I realize sadly. I was on the verge of a beautiful love story and it all got snatched away from me before it even had a chance to begin. Tears stream down my face when I think of what is about to happen—that I'm going to die alone and then my poor brothers are going to find my body hanging in this godforsaken barn.

I don't want to be by myself when the trap door opens. I've never felt so out of hope, so desolate. It's the worst feeling in the world, but I have no control over my fate, at this point. All I can do is pray for a miracle.

My gaze lifts, focusing in on the final minutes I have left and I think about Damon and our time together. There's nothing left I can do to save myself; all I can do is find peace with my situation. And, if I'm going out of this world, it will be with thoughts of Damon on my mind.

I love him.

Pure, bright, beautiful love fills me, and the revelation hits me. I knew that I was falling for him, but the realization is strong and unwavering. Yes, it all happened fast, but I don't regret one moment we spent together. He showed me what it's like to be desired, protected, cared for, and I will be forever grateful for those amazing moments we shared together up at his cabin. He made me feel like a true woman for the first time in my life and I will embrace that feeling forever.

I'm never going to forget Damon Archer. But I'm so incredibly sad that I can't tell him how much he means to me.

I watch the seconds fall away through blurry, tear-filled eyes. There's no point in crying. *Head up, Carlotta,* I tell myself. *Face your fate with as much grace and dignity as you can muster.*

I'd give anything to see Damon one last time, but it's impossible. And even though I was naively hoping for a future with him that won't happen, I can still surround myself with the precious and few memories that we made in our short time together. Ones that have ingrained themselves onto my very heart and soul.

With a soft, shaky sigh, I resign myself to whatever will happen. A strange sort of peace flows over me, assuring me that everything will be okay. But I'm not sure where it comes from or how that can be.

I look up and see the timer turn to five minutes.

4:59.

4:58.

4:57.

Squeezing my eyes shut, I pray that it will happen fast and be over quickly.

20

ARCHER

Miceli parks the Range Rover in a clump of trees and bushes, obscuring it from the road. Meanwhile, Angelo, Vin and Enzo are driving around and parking in the back part of the property. They will sneak up in a rear attack and take down any guards they find. And the third part of our plan involves the other four families; I just pray they follow through and don't let us down.

As if in answer, a parade of luxury vehicles suddenly drives past us and they boldly pull into the driveway right in front of Gallo's farmhouse which I can see through the trees in the distance.

"Here comes the calvary," Miceli murmurs.

"I think we're the calvary," I say and start jogging toward the barn. "C'mon, let's get my girl."

Miceli catches up and is looking over at me, but I don't pay him any attention or give him an explanation. There's no time and what little time there is left, it's running out fast. There are a lot of moving pieces in this plan, all happening right now, and we need to stay ahead of Gallo if we have a chance of pulling this off and rescuing Carlotta.

"Remind me to pick up this conversation later," he says, but he almost sounds amused. Not angry or upset in the least which is very reassuring. Definitely a good sign that he doesn't want to kick my ass for sleeping with his sister. Hell, it's more than that. For loving his sister.

Time to shelve those thoughts for later, though. Now, it's time to finish this and save Lottie.

"Sure thing." I pull my gun from its holster, and he does the same as we close in on the barn. Gallo had said Carlotta may have an hour or only forty-five minutes before the trap door opens. If we're working with the latter, then we need to haul ass because it's damn close to the forty-five minute mark.

Please, please, please let her be alright, I think. There is so much I want to tell her, so many things I still want to do with her. She has to be okay. I refuse to accept the alternative. Fucking refuse.

We circle around the dilapidated barn and I spot a back door facing the fields.

"There," I whisper and run forward. As quietly as possible, I push the door open and we sweep into the lower level of the barn. Moving my gun from one side to the other, I clear the main area and keep moving.

I know Carlotta is on the second level somewhere and I'm looking for stairs or a ladder. Something that will get me up there.

"No one's here," Miceli states and I nod. No guards, no Gallo, no nothing. But that works in our favor.

Unless we're already too late.

Where the hell is she?

"Carlotta?" I whisper-hiss, searching for access to the upper level. As we approach the other side of the dim barn, I finally find what I'm looking for. "There!"

Running fast, I leap up onto the ladder and take two rungs at a time, my boots moving fast, one after the other. Yes, I'm being reckless because a guard could be up here. But time is nearly out. I don't have the luxury of dicking around. Besides, Miceli is below me, gun aimed up, ready to blow away anyone who might suddenly appear.

Jumping up into the loft, I see Carlotta and my heart falls. Fuck me. She's up on her toes, a rough rope wrapped around her neck, and her eyes are wide in fear.

"Hurry!" she rasps, her body twisting, her fingers clawing at the rope.

I race over to her, swoop my arms around her body then step back off the trap door. Lifting her up, holding her tight to me, I support her weight so it eases off her neck. A second later the door drops and I wobble slightly, teetering right on the edge.

"Holy shit," I whisper, my attention zeroing in on the empty space between us and the floor below. The idea that we just got here in the nick of time makes me hold Carlotta that much tighter.

That was way too damn close for comfort.

"Oh, God," Carlotta murmurs, voice full of emotion.

"Hang on, sweetheart. We'll have you down in just a minute," I assure her.

"Damon," she cries, arms around me, holding so tightly. She's still scared she's going to fall, but not on my watch. No fucking way.

"I've got you, Lottie, and I'm not letting go. I promise, honey."

Miceli appears and I tip my chin downward. "There's a knife in my boot," I tell him, and he quickly drops down and unsheathes it. It's military-issued, sharp as shit, and will get the job done fast in a heartbeat.

Standing back up, Miceli quickly gets to work, using the blade to saw through the rope. I can feel Carlotta's fingers digging into my shoulders. Poor thing is holding on for dear life.

"Hurry," I whisper to him.

"Almost there," Miceli states, working as fast as he can.

Several loud popping sounds pierce the air right outside the barn and I exchange a worried glance with Miceli. No doubt about it—they were definitely gunshots. And that can only mean Vin, Enzo and Angelo ran into some trouble or bad company.

A moment later, the rope breaks and Carlotta is free. I let her slide down my body then hug her tightly to me. "I was so worried about you," I whisper, running my hands down her head and back. "Are you okay?"

"Yes," she murmurs against my chest then pulls back. "Please just help me get this thing off my neck. *Please*."

Her voice has a raspy quality because the rope was wound so tightly around it and I can feel my blood boil. How dare Gallo string up the woman I love by her delicate neck.

The thought moves through my head and, a second later, I realize its significance.

Love.

I love Carlotta Rossi.

I knew I did after she was taken, but I'm surprised at how easily the thought came.

Holy shit. I am a man who is head over ass in love.

But before I can think too hard about what that means, I want that fucking rope off her neck. Together we remove the horrible noose and drop in on the hay-covered floor. I'd like nothing more than to burn the offending thing, but we haven't got time for that.

"I thought I was going to die," she says, her dark eyes bright with unshed tears. I can tell she's already been crying from her red face and my heart swells.

"Not on my watch, sweetheart." I pull her close and press my lips to hers. But before anything can get too steamy, a throat clears and we reluctantly move apart. Miceli is watching us closely and I slide my arm around Carlotta's waist, making it clear that she's mine, whether he likes it or not.

Hopefully we get his—and her whole family's—approval. But, first things first.

"No time for that," Miceli interrupts, his lips twitching as he tries not to smile. "We have a plan to follow through with and an asshole to eliminate. Plus, those were gunshots and they might need some backup."

"Roger that," I say, my voice firm, steady and full of determination. Right now, my part of the plan, and my first priority, involves escorting Carlotta back to the Range Rover and making sure she gets to safety. Meanwhile, Miceli will join his brothers and confront Gallo, along with the other members of the Five Families.

We climb down the ladder, leaving that god awful loft behind, and now it's time to go our separate ways and fulfill the plan.

"Get to the car," Miceli says, hurrying toward the front of the barn.

"See you soon," I say and he nods.

"Be careful!" Carlotta calls out.

I reach for Carlotta's hand and pull her with me, back toward the rear exit where Miceli and I came in. "We're going this way, sweetheart," I tell her, guiding her back through the barn as quickly as possible.

The sooner I get her safely back in the SUV, the better I'll feel. Because right now I have the strangest feeling that we're walking on a landmine—and, at any second, we could run into a hidden bomb and be blown to hell.

Maybe I'm just being paranoid, but my gut is screaming a warning at me to be careful. And this time, I'm going to listen.

Once we reach the door, I make sure Carlotta is safely behind me, then carefully open it and peer outside. The coast looks clear, so whatever was happening earlier is over. Most likely, the Rossi brothers took down some guards and now everyone is inside the house, discussing Gallo's future.

Or, imminent demise.

"Let's go," I hiss and pull her outside. Still holding hands we hurry along the edge of the barn and, just as we're about to reach the end of the building, Carmine Gallo comes running around the corner. Eyes wild with blood running down the side of his face, he's waving a gun.

Shit.

I skid to a halt, pushing Carlotta behind me in case Gallo decides to take a shot. I just rescued my girl from certain death, so I'm not about to let her get shot by this maniac.

When he sees Carlotta, Gallo becomes infuriated. "You should be dead!" he yells.

That's it. I am officially done with this asshole. Lifting my gun, I'm about to take my shot when I hear movement. Glancing over my shoulder, I see two guards move up behind us.

"Don't move," one of them growls, and I freeze.

Behind me, Carlotta makes a soft, mewling sound, her fingers digging into my arm. "Damon," she says softly.

I can hear the tremor in her voice and I turn to see one of the thugs has the barrel of his gun pressed against her back.

"Toss your weapon," he orders, yanking her away from me.

Clenching my jaw, and without much of an option, I throw my pistol aside and tighten my hands into fists.

Goddammit. Where the hell is Miceli and everyone else? Why is Gallo out here with his men? Determined to protect Carlotta, I meet her worried eyes and give her a slight, hopefully reassuring, tilt of my head. I refuse to let anything else bad happen to her. Not when she just barely escaped being hanged.

"Get back in the barn," Gallo snaps.

I grit my teeth, not wanting to return to the barn of death. But, at this point, we don't seem to have a choice. However, maybe I can strike a bargain while we walk.

"Why don't you let her go?" I suggest. "And then you can go talk business with the men waiting inside your house."

"They aren't here to talk business," he seethes. "They want me dead! But they're the ones who are going to die. You all are for what you did to my son…my family."

I have no idea what he's talking about, but Carlotta doesn't hesitate to speak up.

"What happened to Maximo was a tragedy," she says in a gentle voice, "but no one wanted to hurt him. Not purposely. My family would've helped him if they could have, I promise you that."

"Save your promises for someone who cares," Gallo snaps. "The harsh truth is my son is dead and it's because of your family. Nothing will bring him back, but I will get my revenge."

So apparently Gallo blames the Rossi's for his son's demise. I don't know any of the details, but suddenly things are starting to make more sense.

"I thought you wanted a seat at the table," I say carefully, trying not to agitate the man further. We're just stepping back into the barn and he swipes a hand over his cheek, smearing the blood there.

"All I want is to end the Rossi family," he grates out, "and I won't stop until they're all six feet under. Starting with you."

He turns his hateful gaze on Carlotta, pinning her with a daggered look full of wrath. The next thing I know, he lifts his gun and fires.

And I do the only thing I can do.

I jump in front of my girl.

21

CARLOTTA

The moment Gallo lifts his gun and points it at me, I freeze. It's like my feet are glued to the ground and I'm completely immobile. A shot cracks through the air, but before it can hit me, I get slammed into the ground, the wind knocked right out of my lungs.

For a dazed moment, I have no idea what happened. I don't think I was shot because there's no piercing burn, just the pain of landing really hard on the barn's floor. And then I hear Gallo's angry roar, but I don't care. I'm just happy to be alive and not bleeding out.

It takes me a moment to realize Damon knocked me down to the ground, saving me from the bullet. His big body covers me, protecting me, and my heart swells. My protector, always making sure I'm safe and secure. God, I love this man. But then he's yanked off me by the two thugs and a horrible thought hits me.

Did he get shot?

Turning around and sitting up, I quickly scan his body, but he looks okay. Thank God, Gallo is a terrible shot.

He's fuming, however, and a moment later, Gallo storms toward me and I roll sideways as he shoots the gun again. Lucky for me, the bastard misses again. Scrambling to my feet, I see Damon break free from the thugs' hold and launch a kick which sends one of them flying. As he throws a punch, getting into a scuffle with the other one, I realize it's up to me to take care of Gallo.

I see a shovel leaning against the wall beside an empty horse stall, and I make a mad dash for it, weaving as I race over. But Gallo isn't shooting anymore which surprises me. I reach my makeshift weapon, grab the handle and spin around just in time to see a red-faced Gallo cursing at his gun then tossing it aside. It must've jammed or maybe it's out of bullets. Whatever the case, I send up a silent thank you to whoever is watching over me.

Now without his pistol, he doesn't look very threatening and I take immediate advantage of the situation. Stalking forward, I lift the shovel and swing it at his body like a baseball bat. He tries to avoid it, jumping to the side, but I manage to whack him hard against his hip. With a howl, he levels his black, rage-filled eyes on me.

"You're going to die," he threatens me, a hand pressed on the spot where I hit him.

"Not today, asshole!" I swing the shovel again, but this time he manages to grab it. *Oh, shit.* I try to pull it away from him, but he yanks hard, ripping it out of my grip. Now, he's turning the shovel on me and I'm not about to hang around and see how this ends.

While Damon is busy fighting with the other thug, I spin around and race away from Gallo. Since the exit is behind me, my only option is to run deeper into the barn. He's calling my name, chasing after me, but I don't slow down or even dare to look over my shoulder. Instead, I run for my life…straight back to the damn hay loft.

Without a choice, I leap for the ladder and hurry up the rungs as fast as I can. Gallo is a heavy, bigger man, so he's not going to be able to catch me, especially carrying that shovel. Maybe once I get to the top,

I will be able to regain the advantage by being above him. If I can kick him or hit him or push him back down the ladder, I can hold him off until Damon arrives to help me.

The moment I reach the upper level, I scan the area quickly, desperate to find something to use against the madman snapping at my heels. My gaze lands on the rope that had been around my neck but, other than that, I don't see anything to defend myself. And, honestly, I'm not even sure what I can do with it, other than maybe use it like a whip. And that's really stretching it. But it's better than nothing, I think, and swipe it up off the floor.

I spin back around just in time to see Gallo lumbering over the side of the platform. At least I can take comfort in the fact he doesn't have a gun or this confrontation would be over really freaking fast.

Once he's standing up, shovel in his hand, he takes a moment to catch his breath. My fingers tighten around the rope and I adjust my hold, getting ready to spring into action and hopefully be able to turn the tables. Because this time, he is not putting a noose around my neck.

If things go my way, this rope is going to be around his bloated neck.

"What do you think you're going to do with that?" he taunts, stepping closer.

"Whatever I have to," I tell him, bravely lifting my chin, and raising the rope out in front of me. I'm still debating how best to attack and defend myself with it when he laughs, throws the shovel aside, and levels the most hate-filled gaze on me.

"Did you know anything about my son?" he asks, moving closer.

"What? No," I respond, surprised by his question. I never knew who the man was until he'd told me earlier.

"He thought you were pretty." Gallo snorts, his eyes narrowing. "But you didn't give him the time of day."

My mouth drops open slightly, and I'm completely surprised by what he's saying. I can't remember ever meeting anyone named Maximo.

"He told me Carlotta Rossi is so beautiful, but she didn't even notice me," he continues, closing in.

I don't know what to say without angering him further, so I keep my mouth shut and take a step back...and realize I'm way too close to the trap door.

"I'm sorry, but I don't remember meeting him," I say, deciding it's probably best to keep him talking. "But I'm sure he was lovely."

I try to muster up as much confidence in that statement as I can, but knowing Maximo was Gallo's son, I'm not sure if I believe it. He was probably a prick just like Carmine. What's the saying? Like father, like son. And the apple doesn't fall far from the tree, right?

"Don't pretend you care," he hisses. "You're a liar just like the rest of your family. Maximo made the mistake of falling for your treacherous deceit and wicked beauty, but it's all a facade. He tried talking to you, but you brushed him off, didn't even give him the courtesy of a polite conversation."

God, what is he talking about? I rack my brain, trying to remember where we were and who he was, but I can't picture him no matter how hard I try. I honestly haven't gone out much recently. Except for the masquerade party, I've been pretty antisocial since everything fell apart with Rendall.

Which means the last time I was at an event where I might've met Maximo...well, it would've had to have been the Rossi Winery anniversary celebration. It was months ago and my family had organized a huge party to celebrate fifty years in business. My parents visited from Sicily and we threw a huge shindig at The Plaza and practically invited the entire city.

Then I remember exactly. The man who tried to talk to me, but I was too worried about Rendall to pay him any attention.

"The Anniversary party," I murmur, everything clicking in my memory, and Gallo nods.

"Ding, ding, ding. Finally, she remembers."

Just barely, though. I was so hung up on Rendall at the time and he's all I could see. Stupid, but true. I was totally smitten by the jerk, so when a slightly overweight man in glasses tried to talk to me, I was only half-listening because all of my attention was focused on the man who would later cheat on me. Maybe I should have given Maximo more attention. He was quiet and a little awkward, though, so when whatever little conversation we'd had fizzled, we parted ways and I didn't see him again. Never gave him a second thought… until now.

"He barely said anything to me," I say, "and I had no idea he was interested."

"That's because you are a self-absorbed bitch," he snarls and lunges straight at me. I sidestep the trap door then throw myself to the side, sliding across the hay covered floor. But Gallo makes a grab for me and manages to snag a handful of hair. I scream when he yanks me backwards and then he wraps his fingers around my neck and starts squeezing.

Oh, God. I've lost the rope, had to let it go so I could grab Gallo's wrists, and the pressure on my throat is increasing. Gallo looks down at me, smiling like a demented clown as his meaty fingers dig into the tender flesh of my neck. I'm trying hard to push him away, but I can't. He's stronger than me and even when I use all of my strength, it isn't enough.

I can't die. Not when I have so many things left to do and not when I still have to tell Damon the most important thing I will ever tell a man —I love you.

A burst of strength fills me and then I hear Damon shout my name.

"Carlotta!"

I can hear his boots pounding against the floor below, getting closer, but I can't respond because Gallo is choking the shit out of me. So, instead, I muster up every ounce of strength I can and jerk my knee upwards, hitting him right in the balls.

With a shout of pain, Gallo loosens his hold enough that I can squirm sideways and kick him in the groin again. That does the trick. He finally lets go and I quickly scramble backwards. My attention shifts to the edge of the loft where Damon appears and relief floods me. Pulling myself to my feet, I take a step toward him when Gallo suddenly pops up. Without warning, he throws himself at me and everything seems to start moving in slow motion, as though my life is about to flash before my eyes.

Damon yells my name. Gallo's feet get tripped up in the rope on the floor and his arms start windmilling, balance and control lost. I dive out of the way before he can grab hold of me and watch in horror as his momentum sends him careening past me and straight over the edge. Gasping, I slap a hand over my mouth as he falls through the trap door. His brief shout of surprise fills the air before there's a loud, sickly thud from below.

Shocked, I feel Damon pull me up into his arms and he embraces me tightly.

"Lottie, sweetheart, are you okay?" He leans back, cups my face in his callused hands and searches my gaze.

For a stunned moment, I can't speak. Everything just happened so fast. But then I find my voice. "Is h-he dead?" I ask, clutching onto his forearms.

"Don't move," he says and reluctantly releases me. Then he walks over to the hole in the floor and looks down. His expression remains unreadable, but when he looks up and locks eyes with me, I know.

"He's dead," Damon confirms.

"Oh, God." Even though the man hated me and nearly strangled me—twice—I can't find it in myself to be glad he's gone. If anything, I feel bad for him. I think after he lost his son, he spiraled into an inconsolable grief that led him to revenge.

A revenge that he died trying to obtain.

I am relieved, though, knowing that I'm finally safe. My family and I will never have to worry about Carmine Gallo again. It's over.

"C'mere, sweetheart."

I take a wobbly step toward Damon and he catches me before my legs can give out. He holds me up and cradles me against his firm chest, providing me with renewed strength. After a minute of soaking up his warm, vibrant energy, I pull back and look up into beautiful dark eyes swirling with so much emotion.

"I didn't think I'd get this chance," I say softly and my voice catches. "But now that it's here, I'm not going to hold back. I love you, Damon. I think I was half in love with you the first night we met."

"Oh, sweetheart, I was the one who fell for you. So damn hard. And now there's no going back because I am head over heels in love with you, Carlotta Rossi."

The purest joy I have ever known pours through my body and then Damon's lips crash against mine. The kiss we exchange is full of so much emotion and, even more, it holds the promise of a future together.

The pounding of feet below snags my attention and we pull apart, still wrapped in each other's arms as we look over the side of the loft. Down below, I can see my brothers as well as some members of the other mafia families. Everyone's attention is on Gallo's body. A quick glimpse tells me all I need to know—he died of a broken neck.

"Don't look, sweetheart," Damon whispers, gently turning my face away from the horrific sight. I bury my face against his chest, breathing his spicy scent deeply, and then hear a familiar voice. We both turn to see Angelo who just popped up over the side of the loft.

"Well, well, well," he draws out, mouth curving up in a smirk. "What have we got here?"

Suddenly shy, realizing we're going to have to tell my brothers about us, I smother my face deeper into Damon's warmth.

"I love your sister," Damon announces loudly enough for everyone to hear. All attention snaps up to us from below, and I feel my face flush with happiness.

"And I love you," I say. Arms wrapped around each other, I look from one brother to the next, watching them each process what we just revealed.

I'm not sure what to expect, but no one looks too surprised and smiles break out all around. Relief fills me and I slump against Damon. Everything I ever wanted is right here in my arms and I can feel my siblings' approval.

My world is suddenly right again.

"Sure took you guys long enough," Damon complains. "But we handled it. Didn't we, sweetheart?"

I nod and then he lowers his mouth again, catching my lips in a kiss that is so full of promise, so full of love. And I have no doubts that we have a future together.

22

ARCHER

Karma is a funny thing, I think, as we leave the barn. Carlotta is tucked under my arm and, as we walk across the yard, her brothers explain what happened on their end while we were battling it out in the barn.

Apparently, Gallo had evaded capture during the takeover and managed to escape through a back window with a couple of his henchmen. While they searched the house, they were already headed for the barn. I'm not quite sure how he cut the side of his face, but the man was deranged and deserved his fate. Especially after trying to kill Carlotta. No one messes with my girl and gets away with it. Fucking no one.

"We have things to discuss," Miceli states, and it's quickly decided by the group gathered that there will be an immediate emergency meeting of the Five Families.

All I want to do is take Carlotta home and care for her. I know she must still be shaken, but Miceli insists we all go. Including me.

I halt in my tracks. "Me?" I echo in surprise. I am not part of the Five Families and have never been to a meeting. And why would I? I don't even have a family left, much less any connection to these powerful mafia clans.

"That's right. You're a part of what just went down and now it looks like you're sleeping with my baby sister."

"Miceli!" Carlotta hisses. "That's none of your business."

"If this man eventually marries you, that makes it my business. Because then he's family."

Marriage is something I thought was never in the cards for me. Especially after losing Caitlin. The sad truth is I never really loved her. But now, I can't stop thinking about marrying Carlotta. In fact, the idea has taken root and I'm beginning to obsess over it.

Everything that has happened between Lottie and I has been so soon, so sudden, and yet so damn good. So why not keep up with that tradition? The sooner I get her brothers' permission, I decide I'm going to put a ring on her finger. A very big, very shiny diamond ring.

Because I am not letting this amazing woman go. Not ever.

It's decided that the meeting will take place in the backroom of an Italian restaurant where the Rossi's know the owner and are good friends. We climb back into the Range Rover while Miceli makes the call and sets everything up.

I pull Carlotta against me and she lays her head on my shoulder. For the duration of the ride, Miceli, Leo and I talk about what happened at the farmhouse and Carlotta pipes in to tell us what Gallo said about his son and how he had approached her, but she blew him off. She also informs us about how the Holloway deal falling through cost him his job and, in the end, his life.

That was a curveball no one expected. But I can only feel so much sympathy for the man. No one forced him to borrow all that money from unsavory loan sharks. At some point, he needed to take responsibility for his own bad decisions. And if Carlotta wasn't interested in pursuing anything with Maximo then that's her decision, her right.

Once we reach the restaurant, everyone is ushered into the private back room where wine is already being poured into glasses. I hate to think a man's death is cause for celebration, but Gallo was a thorn in everyone's side and his bold attempt to destroy the alliance, the table, and these five powerful mafia families, led to his own downfall.

I can only have so much sympathy for the man. Technically, I have none and I won't mourn his passing. Not after the terrible things he did. But I can see the toll that all of this has taken on Carlotta and I think she might even be harboring some guilt over what happened. We'll have to talk about it tonight and she needs to understand that everything that happened was Carmine and Maximo Gallo's own damn faults.

The table is huge and everyone eventually is present—The Rossi's and their wives, The Bianchi's, The DeLuca's, The Caparelli's and The Milano's. It's a damn intimidating room of the most powerful people in this city, and I'm getting a few side eyes. I can tell some of them are wondering why I'm here and, hell, I'm beginning to wonder that myself.

Carlotta and I sit down next to each other, and I reach for her hand beneath the table. She glances over and squeezes. It occurs to me that I am the only person here not related by blood or marriage. Technically, Leo Amato isn't yet either, but he and Gia DeLucca are engaged and have a date to tie the knot next month.

But me? I'm nobody.

"Maybe I should go," I whisper uneasily.

"Don't you dare," she replies.

"But—"

"Stay," she implores me, and I give in, nodding, willing to do anything for her.

Once everyone is settled, the families get down to business. They've already called in a cleanup crew to take care of Carmine Gallo's body and the fallen guards. The ones that are still alive have already been dealt with—warned to disappear, or more than likely, threatened with a brutal death.

Whatever happens, one thing is clear—there will be no police involvement. The Five Families doles out their own brand of justice and it does not involve law enforcement. Somehow, I guess it's possible because their power and influence extends to everyone of importance in this city.

They've also made it their business to take care of the local businesses and neighborhoods. They aren't just a group of people out to fight and kill and make money off the backs of hardworking locals. They've started organizations that help the small business owners, thanks to Gabriella and Enzo.

Of course, Carlotta has already informed both of them about Maximo and Holloway Corp. I can tell they feel bad, but there's nothing anyone can do now. What's done is done, and nothing can bring back Maximo Gallo or, for that matter, his revenge-seeking father. And, in my mind, that's a good thing.

The meeting goes on for a while and during that time, food and wine are shared. If I didn't know better, I'd say it's a party. But the atmosphere isn't festive; it's all business. I can appreciate how this group has learned to work together because from what I know, things didn't always run this smoothly. Like anything else, there were bad apples and bumps in the road. However, over the past year or so, all of the issues seem to have been addressed.

What I see now is a well-oiled machine and a group of powerful people, working together in a cohesive unit, for the betterment of the city and its residents. But, never underestimate their charity because if anyone threatens their families, they will end you with a vengeance.

Just ask Carmine Gallo. Or Caleb Durant. Or Rocco, Tommaso and Romeo Bianche. They all went after the Rossi family or a woman they loved and not one of them is still breathing.

Needless to say, I consider myself lucky to be on Miceli Rossi's good side, as well as the others.

"And now our final piece of business," Miceli says, looking over at me. "As most of you know, Archer here has been key in helping the Five Families resolve certain life or death issues with my family. He gave me pertinent and timely intel regarding my wife after she'd been kidnapped, and I will be forever grateful to him."

Not sure what to say, I incline my head. Once again, I feel Lottie squeeze my hand and I squeeze right back.

"Tonight, he saved my sister's life and it's a debt I will never be able to fully repay."

"You don't owe me anything, Miceli," I tell him earnestly. And I truly mean it. "I don't want a huge sum of money deposited in my account for my involvement in Carlotta's rescue. Besides, there's not enough money in the world that could equal her worth."

I look over at Carlotta and she beams me the most beautiful smile.

"All I ask is that you—all four of you—grant me permission to marry your baby sister. Because I can't imagine spending a day without her."

A few aww's fill the air and before anyone can respond, I push my chair back with a scrape and drop down on one knee. Then I send a curious glance to her brothers.

"Can I keep going?" I ask, raising a questioning brow.

They all laugh and nod their approval.

"You better keep going," Carlotta exclaims, and this time the entire table bursts into chuckles and smiles of approval.

My heart has never been so damn full and I turn all of my attention on the woman who captured it. My mysterious Queen of Hearts who I know so well now and can't wait to discover even more about her.

"You have my heart, Lottie," I say simply. "And I want to share everything with you."

"Oh, Damon," she murmurs, eyes shimmering in happy tears.

"Damon?" Angelo echoes. "That's his first name?"

"Yeah, who knew?" Miceli interjects with a grin.

"It fits him," Alessia murmurs, leaning into her husband.

"Keep going," Carlotta says eagerly, and more laughter fills my ears.

"Carlotta Rossi, my Queen of Hearts, you made me realize that I'm capable of all the things I never thought I was, and I love you. I love you so damn much for being so amazing. For showing me I do have a heart, even when I thought I didn't, and for filling it with love."

"I love you, too," she whispers.

"Then marry me, sweetheart."

"Yes! Yes, of course, I will!" She pulls me forward, practically right onto her lap, and I have to grab onto the chair's armrests to steady myself. Then I lower my head and we kiss in front of the most powerful mafia families in New York City.

"I think there's one more person whose permission you need," Aldo DeLucca says.

"Yeah, you need to meet our father," Miceli states, holding up his phone to show me the screen where an older image of him faces me. With silvered hair and a strong face, Salvatore Rossi's reputation is legendary.

Even more so than Miceli's or any of the men sitting at this table.

Christ. I rake a hand through my hair, my nerves eating away at me. I'm currently hovering over his daughter and I quickly straighten up, turn to face the phone and brush my sweaty palms down the front of my dirty cargo pants.

"I hear you want to marry my daughter," Salvatore says in a no-nonsense voice. His Italian accent is thick, but his English is flawless.

I swallow hard then nod. "Yes, sir." The head of the Rossi clan exudes such an aura of authority that I find myself transported right back to my military days. If he has this much presence on a cell phone screen, I can only imagine what it will be like to meet him in person. I resist the urge to give him a sharp salute.

Shit. I don't think I've ever been this nervous in my life and Carlotta must know because she stands, moves up beside me and threads her fingers through mine.

"Hi, Dad," she says, greeting him with an effervescent smile.

"Hello, honey." His face softens. "Do you really want to marry this guy?"

Someone chuckles—I think Angelo, that bastard—and Carlotta nods fervently.

"Yes, so very much."

"I hear he came to your rescue."

"Twice," I pipe up. "I mean, two times, sir."

Salvatore looks from me back to his daughter. "Is this true, Lottie?" he asks.

"Yes, Dad."

"And you love him?"

"Very much," she gushes. Pushing up onto her toes, she presses a kiss to my stubbled jawline and I feel my face heat up. No woman has ever had the power to make me blush before.

"And what about you?" he asks, turning his attention back to me. "How do you feel about my only daughter?"

"I love her," I answer simply. "I love her more than I ever thought possible. So much that I refuse to live without her."

For a long moment Salvatore doesn't say anything and I get the sick feeling that he might refuse me. I don't want her father to hate me. To not give us his blessing. Because regardless of what he says, I'm marrying his daughter. But, I'd much prefer to have the most powerful man in Sicily on our side. Otherwise, God knows, I'd probably end up disappearing one of these days, my body never to be found and most likely sleeping with the fish at the bottom of the bay.

"Preferably, I'd like to meet you before you become my son-in-law," Salvatore says carefully. "But I know how careless young people in love can be…and what a hurry they are sometimes in when it comes to forever."

I glance down at Carlotta then back at her father. Suddenly another face fills the screen and I get my first look at Lottie's mother, Carmela.

"Where is my future son-in-law?" she declares. "Oh, well done, Lottie, well done."

I can't help but laugh. "I can see where Carlotta gets her beauty," I say, tossing the compliment right back and the older woman grins.

"A charmer, too, I see," she murmurs, lips twitching. "Just like your father was with me."

Salvatore grunts and she kisses his cheek which makes his stern face crack with warmth.

"Well, if you're done trying to scare off this young man," Carmela says, "I have a suggestion."

We're all ears and wait for Carmela to share her idea.

"Lottie, how would you feel about a wedding here in Sicily at the vineyard?" she asks.

"I'd love that." Carlotta looks up at me. "What do you think?"

"Whatever makes you happiest," I say. And it's the truth. I want whatever puts a smile on Carlotta's face.

"Good answer," Carmela says. "Then it's settled. Lottie and I will talk details and whenever you're ready, everyone is invited to our home to celebrate your wedding."

A cheer goes up around us and then Carlotta squeals and jumps into my arms. I wrap my arms around her, careful not to touch her ass in front of everyone, and we kiss again. In the background, I hear Salvatore gruffly give us his blessing.

Finally, I have everything I thought I never needed. And I couldn't be happier.

23

CARLOTTA

After Miceli hangs up with our parents and everyone congratulates us on our engagement, we all settle back down into our seats again. It's back to business, but after what just happened, I can't concentrate. My head is in the clouds, already planning our wedding, our life, our future.

I couldn't be more thrilled.

How I went from believing I'd lost Damon to nearly dying and losing everything to now being happily engaged to the man I love, I have no idea. Things have a strange and wonderful way of working themselves out sometimes. We're all alive and safe, so I have nothing to complain about. Only a beautiful and bright future to look forward to and I can't wait.

We continue to eat and drink, the mood festive, and at some point the conversation turns, and Miceli says he'd like to get the opinion of the group on an idea. As usual, my oldest brother commands the room with ease and draws everyone's full attention.

"Things have changed significantly within our alliance over the past year," he says and everyone nods, "and I think this is the most stable the table has ever been. We've weeded out the trouble and the weak spots, and we've managed to establish a mutual respect and peace. I believe we've finally found ourselves in a position where we can truly work together to not only better ourselves, but also our friends and neighbors. Trust is something that's earned and after everything we've faced and gone through, I trust all of you and hope you feel the same."

"There were definitely some rocky moments," DeLuca says, glancing over at his daughter, and Alessia lays a hand over Miceli's, "but I believe you're right. It's time to forge our strength in trust and move forward, together as one."

"Together as one," Gabriella echoes, reaching for Enzo's hand. The rest of the Bianches nod in agreement. Ever since Gabriella's cousins kidnapped and tried to kill Enzo, she's done her best to salvage my family's relationship with her family. Of course, their wedding and the birth of little Luna has mended things in ways nothing else ever could have and things have been going extremely well with everyone.

The head of the Caparelli family and the Milano family chime in with their agreement as well. Although coming to meetings with the Five Families is a newer thing for me, I've never seen the table so at peace, so willing to work together. And when I think over the root of this miraculous change, I can only attribute it to love and babies. Well, and weeding out a few bad apples like Miceli had said.

Love truly works miracles and just when I think my heart can't be fuller, Miceli makes his next announcement.

"Since Archer here is about to tie the knot with my sister, I'd like to take a moment and formally invite him to join the table as an official member of the Five Families. It might be Carlotta's last name that's changing, but you're now a part of the Rossi family, too," he says.

"Whether you like it or not," Angelo adds, and everyone chuckles.

"Shall we put it to a vote?" Miceli says and everyone nods. "All in favor?"

A chorus of resounding yay's fill the air, my voice the loudest, and I look over at Damon and smile.

"Thank you," Damon murmurs, his hand tightening around mine. "This is an unexpected honor."

His voice is so full of gratitude and I glance over and can't help but blink back tears. I can tell he's surprised and touched. Our gazes meet as he says, "Together as one," making my belly flutter at the double meaning.

The rest of the table repeats the words and I think we may have a new catch phrase. The coveted seat that Gallo tried to steal now belongs to my husband-to-be. Talk about karma.

And then it hits me. Oh, my God, I'm engaged. I have a fiancé! Last week, I was so scared that I would never find a man to love me, a good, kind, wonderful man who would love me with his entire being.

And now here he is, holding my hand, and looking at me with so much love in his eyes.

I'm beyond ready to wrap things up and take Damon back home with me. Luckily, it isn't long before Miceli ends the meeting and I'm tugging Damon up, ready to bolt. He laughs, pulling me close, and whispers in my ear, "Are you in a hurry, sweetheart?"

"Yes!" I declare, and he chuckles.

After hugging my brothers and telling each one he's my favorite brother, a running joke we have, I watch Damon shake each of their hands. He can be so respectful and I have a feeling it's partly due to his military background. When he called my dad "sir" over the phone, I knew it was a good move on his part and that my dad liked it.

With a wave to my sisters-in-law, I pull Damon outside and then frown, realizing we have to ride with Miceli. Dammit, I wish I had my car.

"Are we going back to your place?" he asks huskily, drawing me into his arms and nuzzling my ear.

"We sure are," I say. "Miceli, let's go!"

I want to get out of here now, not sit around while Miceli politics for the next hour.

My brother looks up from his conversation with one of the Caparelli's and I snap my fingers at him.

"Sorry, I think my sister is in a hurry," he says with a chuckle.

"Yes, I am!"

"Okay, okay. I'm coming," he responds easily.

Damon nibbles on my earlobe and I nearly melt in his arms when he says, "And you will be coming very shortly, too, my love."

Gah. I can't freaking wait to get this man in my bed. After all we've just been through, I'm ready to celebrate life and start ours together. We have so much to discuss and plan, but that can wait. First things first—and that means getting naked between the sheets. Or, wherever…

We have an entire apartment to christen.

The naughty thought makes a tingle shoot down throughout my body and explode in my core.

Miceli and Alessia get into the Range Rover a moment later and he looks at me in the rear view mirror, a smirk on his face. "What seems to be the rush?" he asks cheekily.

I toss him a glare and Alessia looks over at her husband and shakes her head. "Stop being a mean big brother and teasing your little sister," she declares. "You remember quite clearly what it was like right after we married."

"What it's still like," he growls, and they lace their fingers together.

"I swear to God, Miceli, if you don't start driving, we are getting out of this car and hopping on the nearest form of transportation I see. A bus, an Uber, the subway, a freaking bike!"

Everyone laughs and Damon pulls me close, tucking me up under his arm. "Patience, sweetheart," he whispers, pressing a kiss to my temple. "We'll be home before you know it. And then we're going to lock the door and not answer the phone for the next few days."

"Sounds good to me," I say, snuggling up against his warm side.

The ride to my place seems to take longer than usual, but it's only because I'm champing at the bit to rip Damon's clothes off and have my way with him. It's been too long and my need for him has become a physical ache.

Finally, my building comes into view and, as Miceli pulls up to the curb, I'm already opening my door.

"Christ, Lottie, let me at least stop the car before you jump out," Miceli growls.

"You're too slow," I complain, my feet hitting the pavement. "Okay, bye!"

I slam the door shut and hear my brother and Alessia's muffled laughter from inside. Damon meets me on the curb and, after a quick wave, I pull him with me toward the door.

"You seem to be in quite the hurry, Miss Rossi," he teases.

I whip the door open and send him a look that means business. "Get in, get upstairs and get your clothes off, Mr. Archer."

A laugh bursts from his throat and then he gives me a sharp salute. As he strides past me and into the lobby, I slap his ass.

"Good God, woman, I have a feeling I'm about to be manhandled."

I slap a hand against the elevator's button.

"That's right," I whisper, turning to face him. "And I hope you'll return the favor."

"Oh, you know I will," he murmurs, pulling me close. Our mouths crash together in a kiss for the ages. All hot, wet and full of steamy promises.

The elevator door glides open and we're too busy kissing to get inside. As it starts to close again, Damon stops it with his booted foot. Still kissing, he drags me inside and blindly presses my floor.

We can't get enough of each other and, by the time we reach my floor, I'm a panting, needy mess. As we step out, my knees wobble slightly, feeling like jelly. Damon scoops me up and carries me down the hallway as I lift my keys, ready to open that door so damn fast and get inside so we can take this to the next level.

Damon takes the keys from my hand, shoves it into the lock, turns and the door swings open. God, it feels good to be home and safe and with the man I love. He kicks the door shut, locks it and our mouths slam together again as he walks me to the bedroom.

Once we reach my room, he tosses me onto the bed and stares down at me with a feral look in his dark eyes. "As much as I want to go slow, I also want to go hard and fast."

"I have no patience for slow right now, Damon," I warn him. "I need you inside me right now."

"Then that's what you'll get," he promises in a husky voice.

We both start ripping our clothes off and then he's on top of me, our naked bodies skin to skin, and it's so delicious I could almost cry. Instead, I reach for his hard cock and his hand drops between my legs. We're both hot and ready, pulsing and needy, and I stroke his length as his fingers slide into my wet heat.

"Oh, God," I whimper, arching against his palm, riding it as he lightly thrusts against my hand. I have never been this hot, bothered and on the verge of completely combusting like this before. But before we orgasm, Damon pulls his hand away, settles between my thighs and grasps his cock, lining our bodies up. In one smooth thrust, he enters my body, sliding deeply and I cry out.

Wrapping my legs around his waist, I lift my hips and meet each of his hard thrusts. Nothing has ever felt so good or so right. My body sizzles, ready to blast off into the stratosphere.

He tilts my hips just right and hits my sweet spot over and over again until I scream. My pussy tightens and flutters around him, drawing him ever deeper. And as my release washes over me, I swear I see stars. Above me, Damon groans through his release and I pull his mouth down for a long, deep kiss full of passion.

For a long moment, we lay there, our bodies together as one. The feeling of being connected to this man in every way—body, mind, heart and soul—is beyond overwhelming. But in the best possible way.

I moan softly when he finally pulls out and rolls onto his back.

"That was…" My voice trails off because I can't fully express what just happened. It was just too damn good.

"Yeah," he breathes, "it really was."

I chuckle and roll over to face him. Laying my hand on his chest, I press a kiss to shoulder. "I love you, Damon Archer."

"I love you more, Carlotta Rossi."

The weight of his words makes my chest tighten with emotion. "No one ever said that to me before," I whisper.

"I've never said it to anyone before either."

That's right. I remember him telling me he never said it to his old girlfriend. "But Caitlin wanted you to say it, didn't she?"

"Yes. But if I did, it would've been a lie."

Reaching over, I smooth the line between his brows. "What happened to her wasn't your fault, my love. Please, stop blaming yourself."

"I'm trying," he says, grabbing my hand and pressing a kiss to my palm. "You've helped, actually. In more ways than you can even imagine."

"Really?" I arch a brow. "How so?"

He lets out a low breath, toying with my fingers, threading and unthreading his through mine. "After Caitlin died, I thought whatever little warmth and humanity I still had after my years in spec ops died along with her. What I did…it was taking its toll on me. Then losing her seemed to destroy me in so many different ways. I became cold, ruthless and, I thought, completely incapable of love. I mean, I hadn't even loved my girlfriend. I wondered what the hell was wrong with me? I felt like the worst person in the world."

"You're a good man, Damon," I insist.

"I didn't think so." He lays my hand flat on his chest and covers it with his. I can feel the strong, steady beat of his heart beneath my palm. "I truly believed I was incapable of love."

"And now?" I press.

"You taught me I'm capable of whatever I set my mind and heart to—and that love can fix everything. You're a very wise woman, Lottie."

I smile. "So I've been told."

"Thank you, sweetheart," he whispers. "For fixing me in every way that's important."

"And thank you right back," I tell him. "I never thought I'd find someone and I was on the verge of giving up. You make my life more beautiful, infinitely better, in so many ways."

"I'm just glad your family accepted me so easily."

"They've always liked you because whenever the shit hit the fan, you were right there to help us. It doesn't matter your original reasons for doing it. You never let us down, Damon, and we all will be forever grateful to you."

He lifts my hands and presses a kiss to each one of my knuckles. "Let's get you a ring this week. The biggest, most expensive diamond you want, sweetheart."

"I don't need a big diamond, Damon," I whisper, looking into his dark eyes. Eyes so full of love. "I just need you."

"That's nice to hear, but I'm going to make sure there's a rock sitting on your finger. I need it very visible and very apparent, so it will let every other man out there know that you're taken. Because you belong to me now, Carlotta Rossi, and I am never letting you go."

"Fine by me," I whisper. A love like I've never known before fills me and our mouths meld together in a kiss full of promise.

I've finally found my person, my other half, and I'm glad he's never letting me go because the feeling is mutual.

Damon Rossi is all mine and I couldn't be more thrilled.

24

ARCHER

People always say time flies, but when you're preparing for a destination wedding, the saying takes on a whole new meaning. In our case, time has disappeared in the blink of an eye. But every single moment we've spent together is precious. I really couldn't love Carlotta more and each day with her is a new adventure.

One I always look forward to.

I'm a laid back kind of guy when it comes to wedding details, so I tell her to choose exactly what she wants. Guns and ops, on the other hand, I need to know every minute thing down to the letter. Even though I tell her to pick the flowers and foods and decorations she wants most, Carlotta makes sure to include me in everything.

"This is your day, too," she tells me.

"I know, sweetheart, and I love that you want my opinion, too. But I just want you to be happy."

"Damon, we could get married at the courthouse tomorrow and I'd be okay with it."

God, I love this woman.

The plan is to spend a few extra weeks in Sicily. We're arriving early to take care of the final wedding details and then we will spend the rest of the month with her family and celebrate Christmas. After that, I'm taking my beautiful bride on a flight across the Ionian Sea and we're going to honeymoon in the beautiful Ionian Islands off the coast of Greece.

I honestly can't say I've ever looked forward to something as much as the two weeks we'll have alone, just us, exploring the islands and relaxing and having so much sex we might possibly die by orgasm. Maybe we'll even explore the mainland, too. Whatever she wants to do. As long as there's a bed nearby, I'm good.

Before we know it, we're on the Rossi family's private jet, heading over to Sicily. Angelo and Blake decided to come over early, too, and it's nice to have the company. I like Carlotta's youngest brother a lot because he's always telling a funny story and making us laugh. I think out of all her brothers, she and Angelo are the most alike.

Blake, Angelo's wife, is expecting twins, so they thought it would be nice to head over early and let her relax. She's getting bigger every day and is doing well, but I can't say I envy them. One baby would be hard enough. But two? This won't be the only set of twins, either. Vin and Hannah have twin girls—Rosa and Bianca—who are sweet little angels. But, I have to say, knowing that twins run in their family makes me a little nervous.

The plane ride over to Sicily goes fast because we talk most of the way. I've never been to Sicily and neither has Blake, so we're both looking forward to it.

"You're going to love it," Carlotta gushes. "December in Sicily is the most beautiful time of the year."

"You've told me so much and now I can't wait to see it with my own eyes."

"I'm going to take you all over so you can experience everything," she tells me, squeezing my hand.

The only thing I'm a little nervous about is meeting her parents. Maybe it's silly, and I know I already have her father's permission via phone, but I have an old school heart and I really want to make sure he's okay with me. With us. The last month has been such a whirlwind and the way we swept into each other's lives might make him start second-guessing my true intentions.

I love Carlotta more than anything in this world, though, and I will make sure both of her parents know that.

After landing safely at the small airport, Angelo and I grab all the luggage while the women go down to check on the car.

"Are you ready for this?" Angelo asks, looking over at me as I load my arms with as much baggage as possible.

I pause and glance over at him. "Ready for what? Marriage?"

"For all of it, bro! You're marrying my firecracker of a sister, becoming a part of a big, crazy family, about to meet my parents, on the verge of probably becoming a father—"

"Whoa," I hold up a hand and laugh. "Are you trying to freak me out? One thing at a time, please."

I laugh, but I know he's right. It is a lot of change to happen in such a short amount of time.

But, I'm ready. Actually, I've never been more ready. For the first time in a very long time, I have so many new and exciting things to look forward to. I have been solely focused on business for as long as I can remember, and my personal life suffered badly—to the point where I believed I couldn't have a serious relationship or anything beyond that. But, Carlotta taught me I could and that I have so much more to offer than I ever realized.

"I think you're just projecting," I joke, "because your wife is about to have twins and that's a lot to take on all at once."

"Aww, hell, Archer, now you're gonna freak me out."

We laugh as we maneuver the luggage out the door and down the roll away steps. It's nice to have a male friend to talk to about things. Although I had my team of guys while I was in the military, we lost touch when they all moved on and started families. But Angelo and I seem to have a lot in common and get along well which is cool.

We load up the luggage into the waiting SUV. The girls are chattering about all their plans, and there's still more luggage to get so Angelo and I make a second trip. I think the only thing Carlotta didn't pack was the kitchen sink.

"Sweetheart, you sure don't travel light," I comment, finally sinking into the seat beside her once we're all ready to go.

She throws her head back and laughs. "Better get used to it. Even if this weren't a destination wedding, I still like to bring all the things. You just never know what you might need."

I smirk then lean in and kiss her.

It doesn't take long to arrive at her parent's house, and that description is an understatement. The enormous home, surrounded by endless vineyards, is more of a sprawling country villa. It's gorgeous and possesses an old world charm that makes you want to open up a bottle from the Rossi's private wine cellar, sit out on the back patio and soak up all the vibes. Plus, it's decked out for the holidays. Too many poinsettias to count sit on the large porch, wreaths cover every window and I can see lights strung from the trees. I bet it looks spectacular at night.

It's also a bit intimidating and Carlotta must notice my nerves because she reaches over and lays a reassuring hand on my arm. "Don't be nervous," she whispers. "They're going to love you."

I look down at her graceful fingers and see the big square-cut diamond flashing there. It's impossible not to notice. When we went ring shopping, it practically jumped out of the case and demanded to be bought. And even though she claimed she didn't need a rock the size of New York state, I could tell she loved it. So I bought it for her and she lit up like the Fourth of July. She told me she's never taking it off and, as far as I know, she hasn't once since I put it on her finger.

Now, I'm going to add a wedding band and seal the deal. I can hardly wait. *Who the hell am I?* I wonder, stifling a chuckle. *Oh, yeah, I'm a man in love.* Desperately, head over heels, do-anything-to-make-her-happy in love.

As we're getting out of the SUV, the double front doors swing open and I get my first look in person at Salvatore and Carmela Rossi. And my shoulders relax, the anxiety disappearing as Carmela hurries over and hugs me before anyone else. Then she hugs Blake. Then her children.

I'm not sure what Carlotta has told her mom about me during their private phone calls, but the fact that she came to me first and threw her arms around me without hesitation makes my chest tighten with emotion. As silly as it sounds, I needed that. The reassurance, the acceptance, the love…it all means so much to a guy who no longer has any family or friends left in his life. Well, had, I remind myself. Because now my life is so full it's practically bursting.

"Just so you know," Carmela says, "I'm calling you Damon, not Archer like my boys do."

I laugh. "You may call me whatever you like," I respond and wrap an arm around Carlotta's waist, tugging her near. I need her beside me, need to feel her warmth and support. Meeting her parents is a big deal and I don't want to screw it up.

"Mom, Dad, I'd like you to meet Damon—officially," she adds, and everyone chuckles.

"It's an absolute pleasure," Carmela says. Then she lowers her voice and leans toward her daughter, as though imparting a secret. But, of course, I can still hear her. "Oh, Lottie, he's even more handsome in person."

My lips twitch at the compliment.

Salvatore extends his hand and we shake. "Welcome to the family, Damon," he says.

"Thank you, sir."

"Call me Sal like everyone else," he invites in a gruff voice. His attention slides over to Blake. "And how're you and my grandbabies doing?"

Blake rounds a hand over her protruding stomach. "They're kicking now."

"And keeping her up all night," Angelo adds, pressing a kiss to her temple.

"Well, come on in and let's get your feet up. Mela just baked cookies. There's fresh limoncello and we have a special non alcoholic spritzer for you, Blake. And whoever else may be interested."

He casts a side-eyed look at Carlotta and I swallow hard, not missing his meaning. But Salvatore is a man who doesn't mince words or hold back.

"The sooner you two start giving us grandbabies, the better," he states.

"Dad! Can we at least get married first?" Carlotta exclaims, and I chuckle. The Rossi family definitely knows how to keep things lively.

"We're practicing," I murmur.

"Oh, I'm sure you're practicing quite a lot," Angelo interjects.

"Shut it, Ang," Carlotta says, but she's grinning from ear to ear. "C'mon, I'll show you where we're staying."

She tugs me down the long hallway lined with windows and I can only imagine how nice it must be in the summer months with the windows open and the breeze blowing in from the vineyard.

"This place is amazing," I say.

"Not half as amazing as you."

We reach a room and she pulls me inside, closing the door swiftly. Before I can even look around, she throws herself at me, kissing me hard. My arms automatically wrap around her, lifting her up, and her legs circle my waist. After a very long and passionate kiss, our mouths break apart.

"I've been wanting to do that for hours," she states breathlessly, and I smirk.

"Oh, yeah?"

She nibbles on my lower lip, sliding her hand down between our bodies to cover my already hard dick. When she lightly squeezes, I groan.

"You're playing with fire, sweetheart," I warn her.

"I'm ready to burn," she whispers, releasing her hold and grinding against me. "And, hey, we have my dad's approval, so we may as well have some fun."

I chuckle. "Well, in that case, I don't want to disappoint my new father-in-law."

"I don't suggest it."

Turning, I toss Carlotta onto the bed. If she wants me, then she will have me. Without warning, I jump on top of her—carefully, of course—and kiss the daylights out of her.

Ah, I have a feeling Sicily is going to be wonderful in so many ways.

And, it is. Every single moment we spend with Carlotta's family is beautiful. By the time the whole crew arrives for the holiday, I feel like I've known this family forever. They're so warm and welcoming, overflowing with joy, love and laughter. Sometimes, I have to pinch myself because I can't believe it's real.

There's Miceli, a pregnant Alessia and little Nico; Vin, Hannah and their little girls, Rosa and Bianca; Enzo, Gabriella and baby Luna; Angelo and poor Blake who has evening sickness at six o'clock on the dot every night; Salvatore and Carmela, of course, and us. Going from no family to a big circle of relatives like this has been the easiest and best thing. I worried it might be a little daunting, but they've welcomed me with open arms.

On the eve before our wedding, Carlotta and I take another stroll through the village to admire the Christmas decorations and visit the festive markets. Lights and poinsettias are everywhere and we pause to admire the live nativity scenes which she calls *presepi viventi*. I love listening to her speak Italian. Like the rest of her family, she is fluent and it sounds beautiful rolling off her tongue.

Candles illuminate the front of the church and it's all so magical and quaint—like straight out of some old-time fairytale book. We're both watching the baby make cooing sounds in the manger, and I thread my fingers through hers.

One day, I know we'll have a little one of our own.

"Tomorrow night at this time, we'll be married," she murmurs.

"I can't wait. You've given me so damn much to look forward to, Carlotta. So much more…" My voices chokes with emotion. "Well, things I never expected would happen."

I turn to her so I can look into her pretty brown eyes.

"Thank you, my love. For everything."

"Oh, Damon, you don't have to thank me because you've returned it all a hundred times over. I love you and I'm so grateful for you and our future together."

"I love you, Lottie. More than you'll ever truly know."

Somewhere nearby, the sound of people singing a Christmas carol fills the air. With the lights twinkling nearby and the scent of spruce in the air from the cut evergreens laid out in the manger, I pull Carlotta into my arms and kiss my girl with all the love in my heart.

25

EPILOGUE: CARLOTTA

The next day is sunny and unseasonably warm. I couldn't have asked for a more perfect day to get married. My mom slides the rear glass walls back which open up the entire rear half of the house, connecting it directly to the cobblestone patio. A trellis shadows the patio and it's covered by flowers and vines. A fountain gurgles and there's an archway made of evergreen boughs sprinkled with holly. Damon and I will stand beneath it for the ceremony and exchange our vows.

There's a palpable excitement in the air and I am beyond ready and excited. The girls help me with my hair and makeup, and then I slip into a long, white dress made of the softest satin. Alessia touches up my lip gloss while Hannah adjusts the sprigs of holly scattered throughout my hair which is swept back off my face and in a pile of waves at the nape of my neck.

"You look stunning," Gabriella says, and they all nod in agreement.

"That man isn't going to know what hit him," Blake adds, and we all laugh.

My hands are clutched together and I realize I'm wringing them nervously.

"Are you ready?" Alessia asks.

"So ready. But, I'm nervous," I admit.

"Don't be nervous," Gabriella says. "You're about to marry the man you love with your friends and family right here with you. We're so happy for you."

"So very happy," Gia states. I'm so glad Alessia's sister and Leo came to join us, too. Everyone I love most in this world is here and Gabriella is right—there's no need to stress or worry because this is truly the happiest day of my life.

"Thank you all so much for being here. It means the world to me—and Damon. His parents have passed, so we're his family now."

"And we're so happy to welcome him into the fold," my mom says and hugs me.

I feel the prick of tears, but I can't let myself cry or I'll ruin my makeup.

"Don't even think about crying," Alessia warns me, and I crack a smile.

"I won't. At least, not yet."

"At least wait until after you say 'I do' and then I can touch you up."

"Okay," I say with a chuckle.

"Hey!" Angelo calls from out in the hallway. "Everybody decent in there?"

"Yes!" I call back and my brother strolls in, hands in his pockets, looking beyond handsome in his suit. He takes one look at me and whistles under his breath.

"Damn, sis, Archer is one lucky man."

"Thank you," I whisper, tears threatening again.

"Don't you dare cry," he says, and everyone laughs.

"I won't!"

He gives me a hug then nods to the back patio. "Your man is waiting. Are you ready?"

I nod my head. "I'm ready."

"Don't forget your bouquet!" Hannah hands me the small arrangement of evergreen and holly, interspersed with white roses and mistletoe. It's perfect and I take it from her with a grateful smile.

Then Angelo offers his arm and escorts me out into the hallway while the girls and my mom wish me another round of good luck and go take their seats.

My dad waits for me and Ang hands me over. "See you up there," he says with a wink.

"You look lovely," my dad says and I smile.

"Thanks, Dad."

"C'mon," he says, tucking my arm through his. "Let's go get you hitched. I want to see my baby girl marry the man she loves. I also want some of that delicious-looking wedding cake."

Laughing, I grin as the low strains of music fill the air. "Let's do this."

A soft breeze rustles the loose strands of hair around my face as we step onto the patio. My gaze goes straight to the arch where my own Archer waits looking beyond handsome in a black suit. Miceli stands beside him, serving as his best man, and Angelo waits for me. Instead of a bridesmaid, I asked Ang if he'd be my bridesman and he'd said he'd be honored.

My dad leads me down the aisle and the closer I get to Damon, the more fast and hard my heart pounds. This is it. The moment every little girl dreams of. I'm so happy to be able to celebrate this moment with the people I love most in the world. As we pass my family, I see Vincentius and Enzo, all my brothers wives, their kids, and this moment couldn't be more perfect.

My gaze lands on Damon. That man is *beyond* perfection. When we reach him beneath the beautiful arch, he gives me an appreciative, sweeping look and a gorgeous smile. My dad hands me over saying, "Take care of my daughter."

"I will, sir," he promises.

With my hand in Damon's, he takes another moment to admire me again then whispers, "You look so beautiful, Carlotta."

"And you look very handsome," I tell him.

The priest at my parent's church waits to marry us and I can feel my cheeks start to hurt because I'm smiling so hard. Together, we turn to face him and it seems like I barely take a breath before we're exchanging wedding vows.

As we face each other, my hands tremble slightly and Damon gives them a little shake. "Want me to go first?" he asks, and I nod gratefully.

I can feel everyone watching us and to help let go of my nerves, I focus on Damon's dark, sparkling eyes and tune out everything but his beautiful words.

"From the second I saw you at the masquerade party, I was intrigued. You captured my full attention from that very first moment…and now you've captured my heart. I know everything between us has happened so fast, but nothing has ever felt so right."

My heart fills and I can feel a wet sheen cover my eyes.

Oh, well. I guess crying was unavoidable when the man I love is professing his feelings to me in front of everyone.

"You have no idea how much I love you, sweetheart, and how grateful I am. You saved me from a very lonely future…one I thought was unavoidable. You've given me a family again….and a reason…a purpose. I can never thank you enough, but I'm going to spend the rest of my life trying. I love you, Lottie, my Queen of Hearts, my forever."

Sniffling, I lose the battle against my tears when they begin to leak from my eyes. Damon reaches over and wipes them away. Pulling in a shaky breath, I know it's now my turn.

"Damon, I-refuse-to-call-you-Archer—" I begin and chuckles fill the air, "you are the most amazing man I have ever met. You never hesitated to protect me and when I needed rescuing…twice…you came running. Thank you, my love."

"I will always rescue you," he whispers, and I squeeze his hands.

"The night of the masquerade party, I had a feeling that I might meet someone special. Little did I know it would lead to the adventure of a lifetime, but it also gave me the love of a lifetime. And I wouldn't change a thing. I love you, Damon, and I'm so excited to share more adventures with you."

Angelo taps me on the arm and hands me Damon's wedding band while Miceli hands Damon my ring. After exchanging our vows and placing the rings on each other's fingers, we are declared man and wife.

"You may now kiss your bride," the priest says.

Damon wraps his arms around me, bends me backwards, and kisses me. Endless love and joy flood through me and I hold on tight as our mouths meld, sealing our promise to love each other forever. Cheers erupt and then Damon pulls me back up, lifts me right off the ground and kisses me again. Everyone laughs and whistles pierce the air.

When he finally puts me down, I feel positively giddy. Holding hands, we start down the little cobblestone pathway as everyone continues to cheer and toss rose petals. At the end of the little aisle, he picks me up again and spins me in a circle. I throw my head back and laugh, knowing that I will remember this moment for the rest of my life.

"C'mon!" Angelo shouts and slaps Damon on the back. "Let's get this party started!"

We all head back into the house where the food has been set up—a big traditional Italian dinner, of course. Everyone sits at the large table and I couldn't have asked for a better evening. The laughter, the conversation and the wine flows.

After dinner, Damon and I cut the wedding cake and it's absolutely delicious. Nothing can beat my mom's homemade almond vanilla cake. Vin is in charge of taking pictures and he's been snapping away like crazy. Damon feeds me a forkful of white fluffy cake and then I return the favor while Vin captures the moment.

A mixture of Christmas songs sung by jazz greats pours through the speakers which are scattered throughout the first floor and, at some point, Damon and I share our first dance as husband and wife.

"Are you happy?" he asks, tightening his arms around my waist.

"Are we talking on a scale of one to ten?" I tease.

"Sure," he says with a laugh.

"Then I'm currently hovering at a million," I declare.

"Good. Me, too."

Our lips meet in another kiss and the energy between us turns sizzling fast. When we finally break apart, I decide it's time to go. "Are you ready to start our honeymoon, Mr. Archer?" I ask and playfully tug on his tie.

"God, I thought you'd never ask."

As wonderful as our day has been and this entire time spent at my parents' house, I'm ready to begin my life with Damon. We say our goodbyes amidst hugs and teasing then grab our bags and head to the SUV which will take us straight to the airport and the family jet waiting to fly us to the Ionian Islands.

"I have never been so happy in my entire life," I tell Damon once we're situated on the plane. "And it's all because of you."

"I love you, sweetheart, and I think the best is yet to come," he whispers, leaning in to kiss me. It's slow, seductive and so hot my toes curl.

And Damon is right. Our time on the Ionian Islands is full of bonding, exploring and endless sex that is so damn good, I know that I will never forget it. We decide to find a new place to live and not long after we return to New York, I discover I'm pregnant. One month exactly which means I most likely conceived our son while we were tucked away at the cabin.

Eight months later, we meet our baby boy, Alexander, and he looks exactly like his father. Already, he has more charm in his little pinky finger than imaginable and, when he gets older, there's no doubt in my mind he's going to be a little heartbreaker.

The Rossi family has grown even more and I'm so glad Xander will have all his cousins to play with and grow up with. I have a feeling he and Nico, Miceli and Alessia's son, will be close and wreak all kinds of havoc. And, of course, have the girls chasing after them.

On the eve of the one year anniversary of when Damon and I met at the masquerade party, we're sitting together on the couch, drinking champagne, and remembering everything that led us to where we are now. Xander sleeps soundly in the bassinet beside us, snuffling softly in his sleep.

We had talked about going tonight to the charity benefit, but then decided we'd rather not deal with finding costumes, a babysitter and the hassle of it all.

"Are you sure about not going?" Damon asks me.

"Positive," I tell him. "Besides, I have everything I need right here."

"Same," he whispers, taking my glass and setting it on the coffee table with his. He reaches over and pulls me onto his lap. "Now come here and make out with your husband."

I chuckle softly and cup his stubbled face. "It would be my pleasure."

Our lips meet in a kiss that speaks of so much love and promises forever. Before it gets too hot, I pull back and look into my husband's dark, sizzling eyes.

"Thank you, Damon, for giving me the ultimate happily-ever-after."

He gives me a smile and my heart melts. "Always, Lottie."

Then we kiss again and again and again.

And Damon was right. The best keeps coming. I've found my love, my purpose, and I couldn't be happier.

Printed in Dunstable, United Kingdom